AQUARIUS

E.E. LIBERTY

Published by Égalité Press, New York, New York

Library of Congress Control Number 2012939151

ISBN 978-0-9762890-2-9

Copyright© 2012 by E. E. Liberty
All Rights Reserved

No portion of this book may be reproduced or transmitted
in any form by any means
without written permission from the publisher.

This is a work of fiction.
Any similarities between individuals living or deceased
is coincidental and unintentional.

First printing

Printed in the United States of America

Also by E. E. Liberty

Heat, Gin, Despair: Palm Beach Idles

Mark!
I hope you enjoy the adventures of Sabine
Thanks!
E E Liberty

pour l'amour...

toujours,

pour l'amour

ONE

Sabine Jouey slammed the heavy wooden door behind her and turned the iron key in the lock. She strode across the front yard, the grass bright green from last night's rain. Swinging a leg across the silver scooter she snapped on her helmet and paused; the late afternoon light bathed the Provencal landscape below in a soft haze. Hedged by poplars and cypress trees the orchards and vineyards were ablaze in shades of red, rust and gold. The rocky hillside rose up against the blue sky and in the distance Mont Ventoux's peak shimmered like silver. The day was unusually warm for late October; soon the mistral would howl down the valley, slamming wooden shutters and stripping tree branches bare.

    Sabine continued staring down from atop the hill, her thoughts lingering on the past months which had settled into a peaceful routine—sleeping late, leisurely breakfasts by the pool after a swim, napping in mid afternoon to escape the relentless summer sun and dinner in the cool semi darkness at twilight. She had found a measure of contentment; not happiness, but a dulling of the sharp grief that had forced her departure from Paris.

Speeding down the narrow path to the town Sabine breathed in the air fragrant with apples and rosemary. The second spring had arrived in Provence and today was market day—the cobblestone streets in the village square would be filled with shoppers and the farmers selling their produce.

Parking her scooter next to the stone fountain, its carved lion head spewing a steady stream of water, she waved to a neighbor and joined the crowd. Shouts and laughter, fueled by the warmth and the wine at lunch, lent a carnival like atmosphere to the market. Sabine strolled past the tables, vibrant with color and overflowing with bounty, stopping to buy leeks, potatoes and a bottle of red wine. Stuffing the purchases into her straw bag, she paused at a table piled high with ruby apples and golden pears. A shaft of light blinded her for a moment as she stood motionless in the crowd. Suddenly the sun slipped behind a cloud and she blinked. There, across the square, stood a spectre from her past, a ghost from a life she had buried months ago. Sabine continued staring as the sun reappeared and the apparition dissipated.

Jostling her way through the mass of people she peered into the florid faces of the Provencal locals but he was gone. Shivering despite the afternoon warmth she pushed her way out of the crowd and hurried to her scooter.

At the top of the stones steps to her house Sabine glanced behind her, unable to ignore a feeling of foreboding. Locking the wooden door Sabine dumped the vegetables on the kitchen table and exhaled. Her appetite gone, she opened the bottle of wine and poured a glass. Staring through the kitchen windows as the sun set behind the mountains memories came rushing back—the past that had haunted her these past months, the past that had forced her to leave Paris and take up residence in this obscure town, a self imposed exile in a vain attempt to escape. Fighting back tears Sabine poured more wine and allowed the ghosts to return—Philippe, his laughter, his smell, and that night in Paris…Sabine let the tears flow, watching the sun paint the sky in brilliant swirls of orange and red until it disappeared.

Wiping her eyes she swallowed the wine and strode across the stone floor. Opening the doors to the armoire she picked up a maroon velvet bag and crept up the stairs to her bedroom.

A cool evening breeze fluttered the rose brocade draperies from the open windows. Frowning, Sabine glanced outside at the night sky, pulled the windows shut and closed the curtains. Sitting on the bed she stared at her reflection in the mirror—her eyes were as cold and dark as the starless sky. The warmth and color of the past months had disappeared, leaving only an endless black abyss.

Sabine opened the velvet bag, pulled out the .22 and stuffed it under her pillow. She snapped off the light and curled up on the bed, her eyes wide, like a serpent ready to strike.

TWO

The room was dark, too dark to discern shadow from structure. Sabine sensed a familiarity—the sea, the smell of damp wood, Philippe. She was being rocked gently, rhythmically, lulling her into drowsiness. She tried to sit up but something was holding her down. A voice whispered in her ear, telling her not to be afraid, to go to sleep. Sabine exhaled slowly and relaxed.

Suddenly she was standing on the edge of a cliff. Sabine looked down—the drop was over two hundred feet. Below, the sea shimmered silver, spilling into the pearl gray sky. On both sides of the river bank were tree lined sidewalks, their bare branches black against the horizon.

Sabine held her breath, not daring to move a muscle. Suddenly an explosion propelled her backwards and she lost her balance. Faster and faster she fell, her screams muffled by the wind shrieking past her ears. Sabine flayed her arms wildly, desperate to catch anything to break her descent. She looked down—the sea was red; waves and waves of blood had turned the silver pool into an ocean of death.

Sabine sat up—she was in bed, soaked in sweat. Still fully clothed she ripped off her sweater and wiped her forehead. Reaching for the light switch she froze—someone was downstairs.

Sabine reached under her pillow and picked up the gun. Barefoot she crept across the bedroom in darkness, heading for the stairs.

THREE

Moonlight streaming across the living room floor outlined a form crouching in front of the double windows. "If you move I'll put a bullet in your head," Sabine announced calmly from the top of the stairs. "Stand up and put your hands on your head, slowly," she commanded, walking down the stone steps.

The man, in a black hooded sweatshirt, stood up and turned to face her. She flipped on the light switch and gasped. "Gruber!" she breathed. "So it was you I saw today at the market."

He grinned. "Now may I put my hands down?"

"NO!" she snapped, still pointing the gun at him. "I haven't decided whether or not to shoot you. No one would question it—you are an intruder."

"But Sabine," Gruber cajoled, "your conscience would bother you."

"I don't have one of those anymore," she said

coolly, lowering her gun. "How did you find me?"

He shrugged. "The Company has its ways. May I sit down?"

Sabine scowled. "If you must."

He settled into the cushions of the settee and smiled. "That's better." He looked around the cheerful room, his black eyes behind his glasses as bright as a ferret's. "This is very nice," he decided, "very cozy." He smiled again. "Do you have any bourbon?"

"No!"

"Hmmm," he smirked, "you *have* changed."

"Gruber, why are you here?"

"I am here on behalf of the Company."

"The Company?" she spat. "I told them I was through with all of it."

"Well, you may change your mind—that is a woman's prerogative." He paused. "We have received information that a…catastrophic event is being planned."

"What?" she asked quickly. "Where? How?"

"Ah," Gruber leaned back against the cushions, "so the game still intrigues you."

"Game?" she growled. "Do you think it's a game?" her voice rose. "Do you think that night in Paris…" she stopped. His eyes were fixed on her, absorbing every nuance. Sabine exhaled slowly. "If that's what you came here to tell me, you've wasted your time, and mine."

"Sabine," he smiled sweetly, "it is always a pleasure to see you." He looked her up and down. "This country life agrees with you—you've never looked better," he paused, "and your haircut is very flattering."

"Thank you," she said stiffly, "but it is late, and if your feeble attempt to charm me…"

"Feeble?" he cried in mock horror.

"Is finished," she continued, walking to the door, "I must ask you to please leave."

Heinrich Gruber hoisted himself up from the settee. "I told them it would be a waste of time, that you are a stubborn woman, but I would try." He walked slowly to the door, pulling up his hood. "If you reconsider I'll be lunching at the cafe in the town square tomorrow before I leave for Paris."

"Where are you staying?"

"It's best if you don't know," he grinned, "unless you want me to stay here."

"I'd rather shoot you."

Gruber laughed. "You had your chance in Salzburg two years ago, but you didn't."

"I've changed since then."

"Have you?" he asked quickly, studying her again. "Well, that remains to be seen." He paused at the wooden door. "Did I mention the name of the person we believe is planning the attack? I think you know him—it's Professor Dumere."

Sabine swallowed. "Do you mean Stephane Dumere?"

"That's correct," he said cheerfully, "Philippe's uncle. Ah, yes, but that's all in your past. Ciao," he called over his shoulder as he disappeared into the darkness.

Sabine closed the heavy door, feeling as if she'd been kicked in the stomach. Stephane Dumere, the man she'd met over a year ago, the man who was kind and compassionate, the man who had treated her like a daughter, planning an attack? No, no, she shook her head and walked to the armoire, it had to be a mistake. She poured a glass of bourbon, her hand trembling. Shoddy intelligence…sloppy surveillance; she gulped bourbon, her mind racing. What sort of information had the Company intercepted? How did it implicate Professor Dumere? If she could see the files, question those involved…Sabine paused, staring at the bourbon. Suddenly she laughed, a short, mirthless staccato. Perhaps she hadn't changed that much after all.

FOUR

Sunlight streamed through the double windows across the stone floor to the yellow settee where Sabine had fallen asleep. In slumber her face assumed a softness not present in her waking hours. Her square jaw loosened, her small, full lips relaxed, and the frown lines disappeared. An aquiline nose and high cheekbones resembled faces found in classical Roman and Greek art. Glints of chestnut streaked her short dark brown hair, her bangs falling across her forehead.

The warmth on her face intensified and she stirred. Opening her eyes she looked around the sun filled room, her gaze resting on the half empty bourbon bottle on the floor next to her.

She sat up slowly, cradling her head in her hands. So it wasn't a dream—Gruber, the attack being planned, Professor Dumere. How was it possible… the man she and Philippe had spent weeks with last summer could be implicated in such a plot? Stephane Dumere, the man who had raised Philippe after his parents were killed, the man who had welcomed Sabine into his home and treated her like a member of his family, guilty of planning an atrocity?

She stood up and walked across the sun drenched floor to the kitchen, the stones warm beneath her bare feet. Opening the faucet in the sink she splashed cold water on her face, her thoughts sluggish from the bourbon and Gruber's words. Sabine paused, staring through the double windows at the breathtaking landscape before her. How many mornings she had stood here, gazing at the patchwork quilt of fields, the rolling green hills and white craggy bluffs and Mont Ventoux's silver peak shimmering against the cerulean sky.

How blue the sky is, Sabine thought, as blue as the sea on the Cote d'Azur. Sabine thought back to those days on the Cote d'Azur with him and Philippe; the bright blue shutters closed in mid morning to cool the white stone cottage from the relentless summer sun; the long, lazy lunches outside under the covered terrace overlooking the sea; the evening dinners by candlelight; the laughter and happiness. And the nights with Philippe; the silence broken only by the languid chirping of the cicadas; the soft evening breeze fluttering the sheer curtains; the moonlight streaming across their bed.

Sabine choked back a sob and wiped her eyes. She turned and studied the cheerful rooms that had been her sanctuary for the past months. I've been hiding, she thought, from loss, from pain, from life. But no more, she vowed, her jaw set. No, she refused to believe Professor Dumere was involved. He was the closest person she had to family—it was her obligation to prove his innocence.

She glanced at the antique clock atop the fireplace—it was nearly noon. Gruber would be sitting down to lunch in the village very soon.

Taking two steps at a time she bounded up the stairs to her bedroom and opened the faucets in the claw-footed bathtub. While the water ran she grabbed a bag from her closet and tossed it onto the bed. She tore through her clothing, stuffing the items into the suitcase. Unbuttoning her blouse she pulled open the lace curtains framing the window above the bathtub; the sun had disappeared, turning the azure sky gray.

Stepping into the chilly water Sabine shivered, as

the storm clouds gathered outside and in the distance a rumble of thunder roared across the mountains.

FIVE

"Gruber," Sabine peered through the rain soaked window from the passenger's side of his scarlet Porsche and frowned, "don't you think you should pull over until this storm passes?"

Gruber glanced in the rear view mirror and threw her a grin. "You want me to pull over? Does the rain put you in a romantic mood?"

"You drank too much wine at lunch," she said stiffly. "If you won't pull over at least slow down; it's impossible to see more than five feet ahead."

"You are sounding very much like a back seat driver," he peered at the side view mirror. "The rain does not concern me as much," he paused, "as the vehicle that's been following us for the past twenty kilometers."

"Following us?" Sabine stared at her side mirror. "The black SUV? Are you sure?"

"Yes," Gruber said softly. "I have slowed down twice to give them the opportunity to pass and they didn't."

"Can you make out a license plate?"

"Not entirely," Gruber murmured. "The two men inside look humorless." He paused, grinning. "Perhaps they are friends of yours wishing you a bon voyage?"

"More likely they're your acquaintances, if they look humorless," she said coolly. "No doubt you owe them money."

Gruber snorted as Sabine continued to study them in the mirror. Suddenly the SUV accelerated and was torpedoing down the highway, spraying sheets of water in its wake. The vehicle pulled along side the Porsche as both drivers jockeyed for position on the rain-soaked road. The driver of the SUV swerved, nearly forcing Gruber and Sabine over the edge of the cliff.

Gruber, swearing in German, downshifted as the SUV pulled ahead. "That maniac nearly ruined my car."

Sabine, frowning, threw him a side long glance. "The driver looks familiar."

"He does?" Gruber glanced at Sabine. "How could you see him?"

"I couldn't," Sabine said slowly, "not clearly." She reached inside her handbag. "Pull along side of them; I want another look."

"Are you crazy?" Gruber shouted. "They nearly killed us!"

"And they'll try it again," she said coolly.

"What are you going to do?"

"Just get us out of here when I say so."

Gruber scowled, his heavy black brows forming a single line on his forehead. "I'll try."

Sabine lowered her window as Gruber shifted gears. The Porsche roared down the road, coming along side the SUV. Sabine peered up at the man driving, the raindrops stinging her face. She stared, transfixed, as the man stared back, his face finally discernible. Where have I seen him before? she thought. Suddenly his window lowered and he raised his arm; Sabine lifted the gun from her lap and fired three shots.

"Now, Gruber," she shouted, closing her window as the SUV squealed and spun around the slippery highway. Gruber shifted gears and the Porsche roared off as the SUV careened over the cliff.

Gruber glanced in his rear view mirror at the fireball disappearing in the distance and grinned. "You are a woman of many surprises," he crowed. "I'd forgotten what an expert shot you are; lucky my car wasn't damaged."

"Yes, lucky," Sabine frowned. "I've seen the driver before."

"Really?" Gruber glanced in her direction. "Do you remember where?"

"No," Sabine said slowly. "Who else knew you were in Provence?"

Gruber shrugged. "It was on a need to know basis, but the world we live in is very small."

"The world I *used* to live in," she said sharply.

"Yes, of course, excuse me." Gruber glanced up at the sky and smiled. "The rain is letting up; we should be in Paris by ten."

Paris…the city she had loved at one time, the city she swore six months ago that she'd never return to; Sabine stared at the rain-soaked landscape whizzing by, her heart as dreary and bleak as the endless gray panorama.

SIX

Gruber, sitting in his Porsche parked one building away from where he had left Sabine, waited until the lights in her apartment were switched off before reaching for his cell phone. "Good evening, this is Heinrich Gruber, I would like to speak to the Chairman…yes, I realize it is late but this is important…I am on assignment…thank you." He whistled an aimless tune between his teeth as he glanced in the rear view mirror. Adjusting his hat, he peered through the windows. The boulevard was empty except for a solitary couple strolling arm in arm, their silhouettes outlined by the flickering street light. Wet leaves blanketed the sidewalk and drops of rain clung to the half naked tree branches.

"Hello, sir, I am sorry to call at such a late hour but I have news…you already know?" He grinned. "Yes, of course, sir. Did she kill them? No? Well, she is an excellent shot, one of the best…yes, sir, I just dropped her off," he glanced up at her darkened windows. "No, sir, I don't think she suspects anything, but she thought she recognized the driver…yes, a pity…she's not entirely convinced to re-enlist…you have? Well, that should prove very interesting…yes, sir, I am certain the entire community will have heard about this event by tomorrow morning…yes, sir, I think it was dramatic enough to catch their attention…yes, sir, good night, sir."

Gruber slipped his phone into his pocket and turned the key in the ignition. With a final glance at his reflection in the mirror he turned on the headlights and pulled away from the curb, the wet leaves muffling the roar of his car.

SEVEN

Sabine opened one eye and stiffened—where was she? She stared at the crystal chandelier, her gaze traveling to the antique mirror above the ornate fireplace. She exhaled slowly—she was in the apartment in the sixth arrondissement where Gruber had left her last night. From the massive four poster bed Sabine studied the opulent room, having been too exhausted last night to examine the magnificent chamber. On either side of the fireplace were gold brocade Louis XIV chairs atop an oval Persian rug. The peach brocade wall held two gilt sconces bedecked with peach candles. To her left heavy gold velvet draperies hung from the twenty foot windows. Atop the white marble mantle a golden cherub clock leered lasciviously. Eleven o'clock, she yawned and stretched, lying back against the peach satin pillows and closing her eyes. Perhaps she would sleep a bit longer…

The telephone ringing on the antique table beside the bed interrupted her reverie. "Hello?"

"Good morning Fraulein."

"Gruber, how can you call at such an early hour?"

"Early hour?" he cried. "It is nearly time for lunch! Living in the country has made you lazy."

"Hmmm," Sabine murmured, "perhaps."

"Well, I am glad you enjoyed a good night's sleep." He paused. "I did offer to tuck you in."

"That's why I slept so well, because you didn't."

"Ha, ha," Gruber croaked, "it is so nice that your sense of humor has returned. Since we left in such a hurry you probably didn't have time to pack everything you'll need, so you'll find a few things inside the armoire."

"Why Gruber," she said sarcastically, "how thoughtful of you."

"What can I say? I am a wonderful guy. And the kitchen is stocked with…"

"Bourbon?" Sabine offered.

Gruber snorted. "I'd be happy to come over and check."

"No thank you; my sense of humor hasn't returned to that extent."

"As much as I would love to continue this conversation I have things to do. Feel free to be lazy," he paused, "the car will pick you up at seven."

"Of course," she murmured, her mirth gone. For a moment she had forgotten why she had returned to Paris. "Tell the driver to be here at six."

Throwing back the peach silk duvet Sabine slipped into a robe and padded across the Persian rug. Tearing open the curtains she unlatched the windows and stepped onto the balcony. The day was bright and crisp; after yesterday's rain the smell of damp earth and wet leaves mingled with coffee and fresh bread. Across the boulevard at the cafe a few people were sitting outside, their faces turned up to the sky like sunflowers. In the distance the lush lawns of the Luxembourg Gardens sparkled like a field of emeralds. How little Paris had changed, she thought, since that morning in April when she left. Naked under her robe Sabine shivered and closed the windows.

Across the room stood the massive, dark wood armoire. Sabine opened the doors and took a step back. The wardrobe was stacked from top to bottom with boxes and bags, all bearing couture labels. She paused, feeling like a three year old on Christmas morning. A few things she might need, Gruber had said. Sabine continued staring, unsure what to open first. Hanging separately was a garment bag; unzipping it she lifted a package from an inside pocket. Opening the box she gasped; a single strand of flawless pearls and earrings were cradled in gray velvet. Sabine clasped the pearls around her neck, admiring her reflection in the mirror.

Lifting the ivory satin hanger she tore away the tissue paper and beheld the most exquisite dress she had ever seen; black silk as fragile as the paper it had been wrapped in, V neck, cap sleeves, tasteful and elegant in cut and style.

Sabine held the dress against her and stared at herself in the mirror—her cheeks were flushed, her eyes sparkling as the flawless pearls and the black silk shimmered in the morning sunshine. She continued to admire her reflection, twisting and turning before the Louis XIV mirror as light flooded the magnificent room. Suddenly she froze, realizing the significance of the ensemble—this was her costume for the evening, her dinner with The Chairman.

She continued staring, her face drained of color. Then she laughed shortly—their seduction had begun.

Frowning, Sabine threw the dress and pearls onto

the bed. Slamming shut the armoire doors she strode to the kitchen, suddenly ravenous.

EIGHT

"Stop here," Sabine commanded from the back seat of the limousine. She glanced at her wrist watch as the driver pulled over and turned off the engine. He walked to her door and opened it and she stepped out onto the grass. Sabine walked down the quai to the Seine, her high black heels clicking against the wooden planks, and stopped where Philippe's houseboat had been moored. The gray waves lapped the riverbank as she stood, head bowed, and let that terrible night return.

The sun was setting that April evening when she and Philippe sat down to dinner, the galley on his houseboat flooded with crimson from the skylights. Sabine lit the candles as Philippe, wearing an apron and oven mitts, removed the cassoulet from the oven and placed it on the table with a flourish. Pouring red wine into her glass he smiled down at her.

Earlier that day Philippe had announced with great fanfare that he was christening his houseboat in her honor. He sat on the riverbank as she watched him paint, in red letters, 'Sabine' on the port side of his boat. "Now, Monsieur," she gazed down at him, "you are stuck with me."

"Unless I scuttle the boat," he grinned up at her as she pretended to push him into the river. He grabbed her and they both fell onto the grass, laughing.

Four hours later Sabine stared up at him, thinking how handsome he was, his cheeks flushed, his dark hair curling on his forehead from the heat of the oven. "Monsieur," she said sternly, "please remove your apron; otherwise I cannot take your cooking seriously."

Philippe laughed and tossed the apron onto a chair. "Is there any more clothing Madame wishes me to remove?"

"That depends on the cassoulet."

He laughed again and lifted his wine glass. "To the 'Sabine,'" he gazed at her, smiling, "may it weather any storm."

They lingered over dinner until moonlight flooded the room and the sky above them glittered with stars. After coffee Philippe rose and walked across the room. "Madame," he bowed stiffly as soft music filled the air, "would you honor me with a dance?"

She looked at him and arched an eyebrow. "Frank Sinatra?"

Philippe shrugged. "I am a traditionalist."

Sabine laughed and stood up. Swaying to the music, they moved slowly across the wooden floor in the flickering candlelight, their bodies familiar with each other. Sabine buried her face in his chest, breathing in his smell. "Philippe…"

Philippe stopped and stood staring at her studying her face, a half smile on his lips. "Mon coeur," he bent and kissed her, gently at first and then the gentleness disappeared. He looked at her and he was no longer smiling. With one swift motion he picked her up and carried her to the bed.

"Philippe," she murmured, "I love you."

"Mon amour," he whispered, kissing her neck. Suddenly his body stiffened and he sat up, his face grim. He stared through the porthole and stood up.

"Philippe," she watched him as he strode across the room and bounded up the stairs, "what is it?"

"Stay here," he called over his shoulder.

Sabine paused, her mind foggy from the wine and the love making. She heard Philippe shouting and another voice shouting back. Racing up the steps she saw Philippe, who was standing on the edge of the deck staring at the riverbank. She peered into the shadows following his gaze. "Philippe…"

He whirled around, his face savage. "Sabine, I told you to stay downstairs!"

Suddenly an explosion ripped through the darkness; Sabine thought it was a firecracker until she saw the blood. "Philippe!" she screamed. He stood, staring at her, until a second explosion propelled him over the side of the boat and into the river.

"Philippe!" she shrieked, peering into the murky waves. "Philippe," she tore off her sweater and jumped into the water.

The rest of the evening was a blur of police, sirens and searchlights. She had been lifted into a boat and wrapped in a blanket, unable to speak. And the weeks that followed; the questions that were left unanswered; the funeral, the closed casket, and the overwhelming numbness suffocating everything else.

Sabine stared at the Seine and allowed her tears to flow. "Philippe," she murmured, "goodbye…"

The driver, standing behind her at a discreet distance, cleared his throat. "Madame, it is nearly seven."

"Yes, of course," she wiped her eyes and took a deep breath. Sabine strode across the riverbank to the limousine without a backwards glance, tightening her coat against the November chill.

NINE

"More coffee, Sabine?"

Sabine studied the Chairman of the Company from across the table, his face half hidden in the candlelight. He was in his early fifties, his square face framed by streaks of gray in his black hair; chiseled jaw, classic Roman nose, high cheekbones. The Chairman was wearing an impeccable tuxedo with the offhand elegance of a man used to the best. No wonder he can intimidate so many people, she thought. "No, thank you," Sabine wiped the corners of her mouth with a white linen napkin. "Dinner was excellent."

"I am glad that you enjoyed it," he leaned back in the rose brocade Louis XIV chair. "I recalled your fondness for champagne and caviar."

"You recalled?" Sabine asked with mock seriousness. "Or did you re-read my file?"

The Chairman laughed shortly. "Madame, I

remember distinctly one particular evening you spent in Prague—the expense report you submitted was outrageous."

Sabine smiled. "The weekend with Philippe at the Hotel Le Palais," she said softly. "We were celebrating…"

"Obviously," he glanced at her pearl necklace and black silk dress, sipping his wine. "I trust the packages were satisfactory?"

She stared at him. "Obviously."

Sabine had been driven to a back entrance of a nondescript building in the eighth arrondissement and escorted to a private elevator which opened onto the subterranean enclave. The walls of the reception hall were draped in rose brocade and a massive crystal chandelier hung from the gold ceiling. Atop the white marble mantle of the ornate fireplace twin gold candelabras flickered in the semi darkness. On the opposite wall hung a priceless 14th century tapestry; below it a rose brocade sofa ran the entire length of the room. Dinner had been served in the salon adjacent to the grand reception hall, a smaller, more intimate setting.

The Chairman studied her in the candlelight. "Do you mind if I smoke?"

Sabine shook her head at the Chairman reached for the cigar box. "Would you like a cognac?"

"I'd prefer a bourbon."

"Of course," the Chairman's lips twitched as he pressed a buzzer on the table, "I should have remembered." He waited until after the drinks had been served and the door was closed before he spoke again. "I am sorry about the unfortunate incident on your trip back to Paris."

"Gruber was more upset than I—he was worried about his car."

The Chairman snorted as Sabine let the warmth of the bourbon fill her mouth. "I understand both men were uninjured?"

"That is correct."

"Who are they?"

The Chairman exhaled smoke. "Our sources believe they are Eastern European." He paused. "Gruber said that you recognized the driver," he said carefully.

"I've seen him before but I can't remember when and where."

"Perhaps you will," he sipped his cognac, "in time."

They sat in silence, the only sound the ticking of the antique clock atop the mantle. Finally the

Chairman spoke. "I trust Gruber has told you why we asked to see you."

"Only that you suspect a friend of mine's involvement in an attack being planned."

The Chairman puffed on his cigar. "The Americans alerted us several weeks ago; they'd picked up chatter alluding to an…event. The only hard facts were several names, two that you know."

"Two?" Sabine glared at him. "I only know one, and I refuse to believe that Professor Dumere is involved."

"Precisely why you were contacted; if this Professor Dumere is innocent then you would be in an ideal position to prove it." He sipped his cognac. "I understand your reluctance to," he stopped, "re-join the Company. I realize that your departure was for personal reasons, but there is something you should know before you make any decision." He paused. "You left because of the death of Philippe Dumere, correct?"

She nodded, unable to speak.

"Sabine," the Chairman leaned across the table, his blue eyes glittering, "Philippe is alive."

TEN

"Alive?" Sabine breathed, "but that is not possible. He was shot…"

"He was shot, that is correct," the Chairman stood up and walked to the marble credenza, "but it was not fatal." He refilled her crystal snifter with bourbon. "Our agents were watching…"

"You were watching us?" she snapped.

"I assure you Madame," he sat down, "at a discreet distance. We knew Philippe's life was in danger and that certain factions wanted him dead."

"But he never told me."

"We asked him not to, as not to jeopardize the investigation."

"But the funeral…"

"As you recall it was a closed casket. We retrieved him that night and took him to the Company facilities. He spent several weeks recuperating."

"But, but," Sabine shook her head, "why didn't he contact me?"

"Madame," the Chairman said sternly, "it was imperative that the world believed Philippe Dumere was dead until our investigation was completed."

Sabine glared at him, her eyes flashing fire. "And what has changed now, Monsieur?"

"After his recovery," the Chairman shifted in his chair, "Philippe disappeared."

"Disappeared?" she sneered. "You lost him; he gave you the slip."

The Chairman sipped his cognac. "The Company taught him well. Two months after Philippe vanished we heard rumors of his uncle's plan."

"Alleged plan," Sabine snapped.

"If you prefer," the Chairman stared at the orange flames flickering in the fireplace, his face half hidden in the shadows. "Sabine," he said softly, "there is the possibility that Philippe has gone rogue."

"That is ridiculous," she spat. "Never in a million years would Philippe betray the Company."

"Are you willing to bet your life on that premise?" The Chairman leaned back in his chair, studying her in the dim light. "Philippe is one of our top operatives, with information that would be priceless to enemy regimes. It is possible," he paused, "that Philippe is disgruntled because of the attempt on his life which we failed to prevent, and is assisting his uncle because of it."

"Monsieur," she said coldly, "I know Philippe; he is not vindictive."

"I wish I could be as certain as you are," he sipped his cognac. "I prefer to be safe rather than sorry. The Company decided to initiate a search for both of them, which so far has been unsuccessful. We knew if we could find Philippe he would lead us to his uncle."

"So you believe I will have better luck finding Philippe than the Company did?" she laughed shortly. "After all your deceit what makes you think I will help you?"

"The Company is aware of," he paused, "the affection you had for Philippe and his for you."

"So I am to be the bait?"

"Do not underestimate yourself Madame," the Chairman said coolly, "you are the trap."

Sabine studied The Chairman. "How do you know you can trust me?"

"I can't," he leaned back in his chair. "It is a gamble

but quite frankly we have no other choice."

She narrowed her eyes. "You knew I couldn't refuse, knowing he was alive."

He shrugged. "The Company was not sure if your feelings for Philippe were still," he paused, "as intense." He sat up in his chair and stared at her, like a cat watching a mouse hole. "Well, Madame," he frowned, "what is your answer?"

Sabine looked at the Chairman, but it was Philippe's face she saw in the flickering candlelight. He was alive; after the past months of her living half dead, the chance to see him again…

"Monsieur," she leaned across the table, "what is it that you want me to do?"

ELEVEN

Making her way down Boulevard Saint-Germain under a steel gray sky Sabine felt as if she were underwater; unable to breathe, unable to see clearly, the vibrancy of Paris murky and intangible. Last night the dinner with the Chairman had been dream-like but today his words were a knife in her chest; Philippe, alive…after months of agony, of sorrow, of despair, he was alive. A wave of anger washed over her—why didn't he contact her, to alleviate her suffering?

Philippe, alive and a possible conspirator; no, she whispered, glancing at her grim reflection in the boutique window, I don't believe it. There has to be another explanation; I must find him, whatever it takes.

Sabine turned the corner and instinctively glanced across the boulevard to the windows of her apartment. Her gaze traveled to the front of the Beaux-Arts building and she caught her breath. Lounging against the stone facade was a tall man with dark curly hair wearing a red jacket.

"Philippe," she murmured. "Philippe," she called, waving her hand.

The man glanced in her direction and turned away, hurrying to the corner and disappearing from sight.

"Philippe!" she screamed, running into the oncoming traffic as tires squealed and horns honked.

Sabine raced to the corner and paused; he was ten meters away, heading towards the Luxembourg Gardens, his red jacket a beacon in the crowd of people. She gave chase, half running to keep him in sight.

Past the park benches and manicured lawns he strode, like a man fleeing a crime. Sabine pursued him, over the wet grass and sharp gravel, never taking her eyes off of him.

Around the pool she ran, chasing the streak of red ahead, the Senate building's reflection rippling in the silver water. Beyond the Medici fountain and around the path he sped, the bare tree branches black against the pearl gray sky. Sabine paused, leaning against a tree to catch her breath. Above her the gnarled branches of the naked trees bent towards her, as if to grab her, their tentacles sinister and menacing.

Sabine swallowed and resumed her chase, the angelic cherubs in the gurgling fountain demonic in the waning light. A flock of pigeons, roosting on a stone balustrade, disturbed by Sabine's footsteps, fluttered and flew away, their wings as gray as the ominous sky.

Suddenly a group of twenty schoolchildren on their way to the carousel blocked her path. "Philippe!" she screamed, but her cry was drowned out by shrieking children and the calliope.

He continued on, past the stone statues and landscaped grounds down the tree lined path as Sabine chased after him, the stones crunching under her leather boots. He left the gardens and turned down the boulevard, his red jacket vanishing from sight.

Sabine paused, breathless, and looked up and down Boulevard Raspail; where was he? She swallowed hard; people can't just disappear—he must he here somewhere.

Across the street people were filing into the catacombs museum for the final tour of the day. "Did you see a man," Sabine gasped at the ticket window, "a tall man with dark, curly hair?"

The agent studied her flushed face. "Madame, I see many tall men with dark curly hair."

"He was wearing a red jacket. Did he buy a ticket?"

The agent shrugged. "I do not notice what every ticket buyer is wearing."

"But you don't understand," she cried, "I must find him. I'll buy a ticket."

"I am sorry Madame, but the tour is full."

"Please," she begged, "I can't lose him, not again."

Suddenly a roar of thunder reverberated through the air, the gray sky now black and foreboding. Across the boulevard the door to the tabac opened and the man in the red jacket walked out, striding across the street, heading for Sabine.

She held her breath as he approached. He passed her, less than a meter away, without a glance in her direction as the sky opened and the rain poured down.

Sabine watched his retreating figure, the raindrops stinging her face, and choked back a sob. The man was not Philippe.

TWELVE

Sabine stood as still as a statue as her eyes adjusted to the darkness. Everywhere she looked was shrouded in black, shadows without substance, and then, in the distance, a light flickered. The flame grew brighter as a man approached, closer and closer, until he stood before her, his face discernible in the shimmering candlelight.

"Philippe," she breathed.

He stared at her, smiling, and stroked her hair. Suddenly he laughed and turned away.

"Philippe!" she screamed as he disappeared into the black abyss, the flame grower fainter and fainter, the echo of his laughter mocking her.

Sabine was running, pursuing the light, the grass wet under her bare feet. Slipping, Sabine fell hard on the ground, face first on the cold earth. She jumped up and scanned the horizon; there, ahead, was the faint light of Philippe's candle. Sabine stumbled on, peering into the emptiness, searching for Philippe. Suddenly waves of pain crippled her; the grass had disappeared—she was racing over shards of glass…it was gravel, the sharp stones shredding her feet. The gravel became cold and smooth under her bloody feet; she was in a room, dank and musty, the smell of death sickening and smothering. Philippe was ahead; he stopped and looked at her. "You'll never find me," he taunted as he laughed and disappeared into a maze of tunnels.

"Philippe," she moaned, "please, wait, don't leave me…" She raced after him, a phantom in the shadows, the light from his candle growing dim.

Sabine turned the corner and Philippe was standing in the center of a room, smiling. He placed the candle in a wall sconce as Sabine gasped in horror; she was underground, in the bowels of Paris, the catacombs. Philippe beckoned to her, his arms open, as he stood in front of piles of bones and hollow eyed skulls in the flickering light.

"Philippe," she murmured, taking a step towards him; he grabbed her and she was limp in his arms. He kissed her, bending her back as his lips traveled down her neck. With one violent motion he ripped off her nightgown and pinned her against the wall, the bones cold on her naked back. His eyes were savage as he began making love with a brutality that frightened her.

"Philippe, no," Sabine tried to push him away but she had no strength. He leered at her in the candlelight light, his face demonic. "I'm alive," he whispered in her ear as he caressed her breasts, "alive, alive…" then his hands were around her throat, lifting her into the air, squeezing the life from her body.

"Philippe!" she screamed, sitting up in bed. Sabine sat for a moment in the dim light of her bedroom, her breath rapid, her heart racing, and swallowed hard. Switching on the light she threw back the duvet and slipped into a robe.

Splashing cold water on her face Sabine stared at her reflection in the mirror—her face was ashen, her eyes wide and frightened, like that of a hunted animal. Enough, she whispered, enough.

Pouring bourbon with a trembling hand she swallowed a mouthful and picked up the telephone. "Gruber? Yes, I know it's late…no," she scowled, "that's not why I'm calling…" she swallowed more bourbon, "the meeting with Lanier—set it up for tomorrow," she paused, her face hard, "I'm ready."

THIRTEEN

Twenty hours later Sabine stood in front of Chez Margot, peering through the window into the dimly lit bistro. Opening the door familiar sounds and smells embraced her—laughter, shouting, china rattling, the smell of garlic, bread and perfume. She jostled her way through the crowd to the bar, where the bartender, in a white apron, black vest and red bow tie, nodded solemnly. "Madame?"

Sabine glanced at the mirror where the daily specials were listed. "A glass of the Cote du Rhone, please."

"Oui," he murmured, bustling to the opposite end.

Slipping off her leather jacket Sabine glanced around the room. Chez Margot was just as she remembered; the white tablecloths topped with white paper, vases of fresh flowers and flickering votive candles, the cane chairs and red leather banquettes, black and white photographs on the ivory stucco walls, the soft pink lights lending a warm glow to the bistro.

Sabine sipped her wine, thinking of the last time she was here—it was eight months ago, with Philippe; they sat in the back at their favorite table, away from the crowd and the noise. They had lingered over dinner, laughing… Sabine frowned, her mood dark. Why did she agree to Gruber's suggestion? It was a mistake, too many memories…

"Mademoiselle?"

Sabine jumped and spun around. A young man, perhaps 25, with large dark eyes and a mop of dark hair, was smiling shyly. She swallowed hard; he could be Philippe's brother. "Yes?"

"Are you alone?"

Was he her contact? "I'm waiting for a friend of my brother's."

He nodded. "Your brother Armand? That's me; I'm Pascal."

Good Lord, she sipped her wine, the Company robbed the cradle for this assignment.

Pascal glanced around the room. "I've never been here before; this place is very charming."

"And very crowded," Sabine frowned. "It will be

impossible for us to talk. Let's go elsewhere."

"I live in this neighborhood," Pascal hesitated, "we could go to my apartment."

"Fine," Sabine slipped into her jacket, "shall we?"

Outside the full moon shimmered on the Seine as they walked across the Pont Neuf. The evening was unusually mild for November; couples strolled arm in arm laughing and pausing to kiss, their silhouettes outlined in the moonlight.

Sabine glanced at the couple in front of them embracing and cleared her throat. "Tell me Pascal, how is it that you live in the same neighborhood as Chez Margot and had never been there?"

Pascal shoved his hands into his brown corduroy jacket. "Well," he said solemnly, "I spend a lot of time working."

Sabine glanced up at his sad, handsome face. "Yes," she laughed shortly, "the Company can put a damper on one's social life."

"I am relatively new to the Company."

Impossible, Sabine thought.

"I hope one day," he paused, "to live a more normal life."

"You'll have to resign from the Company."

Pascal laughed and stopped in front of a white building with black wrought iron doors. "Here we are."

He unlocked the iron gate and the wooden door. "My apartment in on the ground floor," he smiled. "I have a lovely garden in the back."

Inside the stucco walls of the living room were painted a creamy yellow. Gold brocade curtains hung from the twenty foot windows. A rust velvet settee faced the fireplace; behind it a sofa table held an antique lamp. Wooden bookcases filled the opposite wall and a rust and blue Persian rug covered the hardwood floor. Pascal turned on the lamp which enveloped the room in a warm glow.

"Very cozy," Sabine murmured, looking at the blue velvet Louis XIV chairs on either side of the fireplace, "Your evenings at home must be pleasant."

Pascal smiled, his face flushed. "Would you like a glass of wine?"

"Yes, please," Sabine slipped off her jacket and sat down on the settee, "red."

Pascal walked to the kitchen as Sabine studied the books piled on top of the antique coffee table. "Voltaire?" she smiled up at him when he returned.

"Oh, yes," he said solemnly, handing her the glass.

"He is my favorite author. Voltaire," Pascal paused, sipping his wine, his handsome face thoughtful, "inspired me to join the Company."

Sabine stared at him, his face flushed, his eyes wide. He looks so much like Philippe, she sipped her wine, it was eerie…

"I believe in a better world, a just world."

"And you think those are the goals of the Company?"

Pascal shrugged and sat down next to her. "I hope so." He poured more wine into Sabine's glass. "That's why it is imperative to stop men like," he paused and looked at her, "I'm sorry; I understand you know Professor Dumere."

"I do," she said shortly, "that's why I'm here; I can't believe that he would be involved."

"Perhaps he isn't," Pascal said softly, staring at Sabine.

Sabine stared back, and a slow flush colored her cheeks. She inhaled sharply. "So what exactly does the Company know about this catastrophic event being planned ?"

"Only that Professor Dumere's name was mentioned, the assumption being that he is the mastermind."

"Assumption," she snapped.

Pascal smiled. "I understand your skepticism; it's difficult to accept when loved ones betray us."

"I thought a man was innocent until proven guilty."

Pascal laughed. "You are absolutely right; forgive me."

Sabine exhaled. "I'm sorry; I didn't mean to be harsh."

"Perhaps some food will improve our moods; are you hungry?"

"I'm famished."

"Forgive me, I have been an insensitive host. If you will excuse me," Pascal smiled, stood up and walked to the kitchen. Sabine piled the books stacked on the coffee table onto the floor and lit a candle, its flame flickering in the semi darkness. Pascal returned, carrying a tray. "I have fruit, cheese, olives and, of course, bread," he announced cheerfully.

Sabine stared up at him and swallowed hard. Philippe, he was so much like Philippe; their impromptu dinners, just like this one. She continued staring until he felt her gaze. "It's rather warm in here," he cleared his throat. "Shall I open the doors to the garden?"

Sabine nodded, sipping her wine, unable to speak.

Pascal unlatched the French doors which opened onto a small garden hidden in the darkness. A wave of warm air wafted into the room as he turned and smiled at Sabine, who smiled back. Suddenly his eyes widened as he continued staring at her. Then he fell face forward onto the floor, a knife protruding from the middle of his back.

Sabine blew out the candle and grabbed the gun from her purse. She crept to the open windows and stared outside; the moon had disappeared behind the clouds, enveloping the garden in a black shroud. She crawled over to Pascal in the darkness. "Pascal! Pascal!" she whispered.

His eyes flickered open, blood trickling from one side of his mouth. "Sabine," he groaned, "don't trust…"

"Don't trust?" she hissed. "Don't trust who?"

Pascal sighed and closed his eyes; she felt his pulse—he was dead. Sitting in the shadows Sabine stared at Pascal, stunned, unable to understand what had happened…Pascal, murdered, but why?

A shaft of moonlight illuminated his body and

Sabine gasped. Grabbing a napkin from the table she pulled the knife from his back and wrapped it up. Stuffing it into her bag she picked up her leather jacket and crept across the room.

Sabine opened the door a crack and looked both ways down the hallway before closing it behind her. She hurried down the boulevard to her apartment, avoiding the eyes of the people she passed.

The knife that had killed Pascal, the knife that she had pulled from his back, the knife soaked with his blood that she was carrying in her bag, she had seen before. Diamond edge and tip, specially weighed for an assassin, its ivory handle monogrammed 'PD'… the knife was Philippe's.

FOURTEEN

"Gruber? This is Sabine…" she frowned, rubbing her forehead, "no, this isn't a social call; there's a situation that needs your attention…Pascal Lanier is dead," she swallowed bourbon, "he was stabbed at his apartment…no, I didn't see who did it…I'm not injured… about an hour ago…when?…yes, I know the place… what time? Very well…until tomorrow…good night."

Sabine hung up the telephone and ran a hand through her hair still damp from the shower. Sitting on the edge of the bed in the semi darkness she stared out the windows at the twinkling lights of the Paris night.

Sabine sipped bourbon, struggling to make sense of the past hours. Pascal murdered with Philippe's knife…was it a message? Not from him, she refused to believe that he was a murderer…why kill Pascal? It didn't make any sense, unless…Pascal's last words to her were a warning, don't trust…don't trust who?

Sabine finished her bourbon and stood up. She walked to the bathroom and unwrapped the bloody knife in the sink. Running it under hot water, she scowled; what if Philippe's fingerprints were on it? If so, then she was an accomplice to Pascal's murder… no, no, she whispered, it wasn't possible. There had to be another explanation. She wrapped the knife in a clean towel and walked to her bureau, stuffing it in the drawer under her lingerie. Glancing at her reflection in the mirror she froze—the woman staring back was the face of a stranger's…her eyes cold, her face hard…the merciless look of an assassin.

A wave of exhaustion overwhelmed her and she fell onto the bed, too tired to turn back the duvet. Moonlight streamed through the windows, shining on the gold cherub atop the mantle who leered at Sabine in the darkness.

FIFTEEN

Gruber waited until Sabine had turned the corner before he pulled his cell phone from his jacket pocket. "Hello? This is Heinrich Gruber," he glanced up and down the boulevard, "I would like to speak to the Chairman, please…yes, he is expecting my call…of course I will hold." Gruber studied his reflection in the shop window and smoothed his black hair with the palm of his hand. "Hello, sir, I just left Ms. Jouey…no, I don't think so, sir…really?" Gruber's eyes widened, "no, sir, she didn't mention that," he grinned, "I'm sure she simply forgot…no, sir, she's not on her way back to the apartment—she is on her way to the office to speak to Boudreau about the Lanier incident…yes, sir, a remarkable resemblance…it is lucky that we found out about him…yes, sir, it appears the plan is working…the next step? Very well, I'll call her this evening…of course…very good…oh,"

Gruber smiled slyly, "it was my pleasure…ciao."

Gruber snapped his phone shut and slipped it into his pocket. He gazed up at the November sky and smiled; the late afternoon sun was bathing the buildings on the boulevard in a rosy glow. Inhaling deeply, Gruber adjusted the collar of his tweed jacket and strolled down the cobblestone street, glancing at his reflection in each window that he passed.

SIXTEEN

"Yes, yes, I understand," Sabine rubbed her throbbing forehead as Gruber chattered cheerfully on the telephone. The past few days were a jumble of questions and confusion, Pascal's warning an incessant drumbeat in her head. There was a traitor in her midst, but who? Don't trust? Don't trust…who was Pascal trying to warn her about? Philippe alive, after months of believing he was dead…Pascal murdered, killed with Philippe's knife…Philippe a murderer? "No!" she said vehemently.

Gruber paused. "What did you say?"

"No, nothing," Sabine exhaled, "please continue."

"I was just finishing. So, Sabine, do you have any questions?"

Sabine froze, realizing she hadn't heard a word that Gruber had said. "I'm sorry; if you will give me the details again."

"Sabine, haven't you been listening to me?"

"It's difficult not to," Sabine said shortly. "Please repeat just what is important."

"Your train to Courchevel leaves tomorrow at three. Your passport and other documentation will be delivered to you tomorrow morning along with your contact information."

"Fine," she said crisply, "is there anything else?"

"We're also sending you a warmer wardrobe."

"How thoughtful. Is that it?"

Gruber laughed. "I hope you like snow."

"I detest it."

"Sabine," Gruber's tone was uncharacteristically serious, "it is important that you are focused. These are ruthless people."

She hung up the telephone…ruthless people… she glanced at the drawer where she had hidden Philippe's knife. Gruber was right; it was important that she was focused.

Sabine swallowed bourbon and stood up. Opening the doors to the armoire she grabbed her travel bag and tossed it onto the bed. She began packing, remembering Gruber's promise of a warmer wardrobe.

Sabine rifled through her clothes, her hand resting

on the black silk dress hanging on the satin hanger. She frowned, remembering the last time she'd worn it—her dinner with The Chairman—then she shrugged. It was still a beautiful dress, she reasoned, tossing it onto the bed, and Courchevel was an exclusive resort; more than likely she'd have the opportunity to wear it again.

Opening the lingerie drawer her hand automatically rummaged for the knife; Sabine froze for a moment and began tearing through the lace and satin until the drawer was empty—the knife was gone.

Sabine sat down on the peach satin duvet and exhaled slowly. There was only one explanation—Sabine studied the bedroom, her eyes narrow.

She stood up and walked around the room slowly, like a tigress circling her prey. Where was it? She ran a hand under the telephone table and over the lamp. She stared at the portrait of the president, running a finger along the wood frame. Sabine's gaze traveled to the fireplace and the gilt mirror, her eyes finally resting on the grinning cherub atop the mantle.

Sabine stood, transfixed, staring into the left eye of the statue—there it was, the lens of a camera. She continued staring, the lascivious cherub leering back at her, and then laughed shortly, wondering which group of ruthless people were responsible for the surveillance.

SEVENTEEN

Sabine stared at the French countryside whizzing by, her mind racing as fast as the train. Three hours had passed since she left Paris and the setting sun was painting the snow covered chalets in a rosy glow. A heavy snow had fallen last night in the Savoie, enveloping the towering pine trees in a blanket of white. In the distance ice capped mountain peaks rose up against the pink sky.

The train blew its whistle, a long, mournful wail that echoed through the Alps. Sabine shivered and burrowed further into her pale blue down jacket, compliments of the Company, and unconsciously touched her left rib, the inside pocket cradling her gun. She glanced at her wristwatch—an hour before she arrived in Moutiers; enough time for a drink in the club car…she needed the distraction of human contact and inane chatter.

A knock on the door interrupted her thoughts. "Who is it?" she called, pulling the gun from her pocket.

"It's the porter, Madame."

Sabine opened the door a crack, the .22 behind her back. "Yes?"

"We arrive in Moutiers at seven; does Madame want anything now?"

"No, thank you," she smiled, "I'm going to the Club Car."

"Very good. Turn left—it is the second car."

Sabine closed the door and exhaled slowly. Glancing at her reflection in the mirror she scowled—her face was ashen and her eyes were as bright as a ferret's. She powdered her face, freshened her red lipstick and ran a comb through her hair.

Locking the door behind her she glanced in both directions. The train rumbled under her snow boots as she jostled her way down the dimly lit corridor.

Suddenly the train whistle shrieked again, and she was grabbed from behind, a beefy hand clamping over her mouth like a vice. Instinctively she jerked her head back, smashing his nose, and elbowed him in the ribs. He loosened his grip and she bit him savagely in the hand. Muffling a cry he dragged her into a compartment and threw her on the floor. Reaching into her pocket she rolled over and faced him, the gun pointed at his forehead.

He froze, his face hidden in the shadows. "Over there," she commanded, motioning with the gun as she stood up.

He hesitated as she backed to the wall and snapped on the lights. "I said sit down," her words were cold and clipped.

He sat down heavily and studied her. "That is a little gun," he sneered.

"But I'm an excellent shot," she said coolly, "would you like me to prove it?" she aimed it at his groin.

He stifled a shudder and said nothing. Sabine stared at him—he was 50, square head, graying hair, heavy set with a thick neck and cold blue eyes. He was wearing a cheap plaid jacket and well worn shoes. She continued studying him. "I remember you," she said slowly, "you were driving the SUV…"

"That you destroyed," he bellowed. "But you didn't kill me."

"A pity," she murmured. "Who are you?"

He shrugged. "Who I am is not important, but

you," he leveled icy eyes on her, "who you are, now that is important."

"Why? Who sent you?"

"Martine La Mirande," he sneered, "that is the name you are traveling under, isn't it Madame Jouey? I ask —who sent you?"

"Who are you working for?"

"Who are YOU working for?" he roared. Sabine continued staring at him as the shadows from the past took shape. His face had been shrouded in darkness that night but his voice…his voice. "You were the man," she swallowed hard, "in Paris, months ago, on the riverbank, who shot Philippe…"

Suddenly the lights flickered and he lunged for the gun. Sabine fired one shot, hitting him in the middle of the forehead. He paused, a look of astonishment on his face, and fell to the floor with a heavy thud.

Sabine bent over and checked his pulse; he was dead. Reaching inside his jacket she pulled out his wallet; a few euros and a Bulgarian passport. Sabine stuffed it back into his pocket and walked to the door, switching off the lights. Checking the hallway she headed for the Club Car; there was still time for a drink before she arrived, a drink to celebrate.

EIGHTEEN

"How was your trip?"

Sabine studied the lanky blonde woman lounging against the black sports car at the Moutiers train station. She was tall, nearly six feet, Sabine estimated, wearing a navy wool cap and white ski jacket. She stared back, her bright blue eyes gazing at Sabine with blatant curiosity.

"Madame Fontaine?"

"Beatrice," she flashed a dazzling smile. "Your hair is shorter than in the picture," she paused, "I like it," she decreed.

"I'm glad," Sabine laughed, "my trip was…eventful."

"Hmmm," Beatrice popped open the trunk and Sabine tossed in her bag, "we've already heard about your…traveling companion. Another agent was aboard the train; he took care of the details."

"How thoughtful of him," Sabine frowned. "I wish I'd known I had back-up."

"It was a last minute decision by the Company; after the highway incident they are being extremely cautious."

"The driver of the SUV was the man on the train that I shot."

Beatrice slammed the truck shut and slid behind the wheel, "You must tell me the whole story, over a cocktail." She glanced in the rear view mirror. "I hope you like your rooms; they're adjacent to mine. You have a lovely view of the mountains."

"I detest snow," Sabine muttered, gazing out at the gingerbread chalets of the Savoie. "I hope you don't expect me to ski."

Beatrice laughed shortly. "No, I'm not that sinister."

Neither of them spoke for the remainder of the trip. Beatrice handled the sharp turns of the winding mountain road with the careless proficiency of one who is comfortable with speed and adversity. She sped into the driveway of their hotel and a valet rushed to greet them. "Let's meet in an hour at the hotel bar," Beatrice suggested, tossing her keys to the attendant.

Sabine breathed in the icy mountain air, the cold dryness stinging her lungs. "Fine."

An hour later, after a cool shower and a quick nap, Sabine felt refreshed. Zipping up the black silk dress and clasping the pearls around her neck, she smiled as she brushed on red lipstick—she was right about this dress, admiring her reflection; it was gorgeous. With a final glance in the mirror she grabbed her handbag and walked to the door. Sabine paused, remembering the .22 in the drawer; she frowned, then slipped the gun into her black satin bag.

Beatrice was sitting at the bar, her long legs in silver stilettos, wearing a blue satin sheath. She smiled as Sabine sat down. "Feeling better?"

She glanced at Beatrice's half empty champagne flute. "Yes, and I will feel even better in a moment," she motioned to the bartender.

Sipping her champagne, Sabine studied her surroundings. The bar was the length of the room, built with dark wood and a zinc top. Fresh flowers adorned both ends and a forty foot antique mirror reflected the opulent dining room. Wooden beams lent a rustic look as candles flickered in the windows and on the tables. A crystal chandelier dominated the dining room, its lights glinting in the mirror.

"The town is excited because of the early snowfall," Beatrice sipped champagne, "they're hoping for a lucrative season."

Sabine glanced in the mirror at a group of Chinese businessmen in suits who had ordered a magnum of Dom Perignon, which arrived with a fanfare of a silver ice bucket shooting fireworks. "It looks lucrative already."

Beatrice laughed, a sharp staccato that revealed white, even teeth, and motioned to the bartender. "Let's have another glass of champagne and then you can tell me what happened on the train."

Twenty minutes later, as Sabine finished the story, Beatrice frowned. "And you say he looked familiar?"

"I thought I recognized his face," she said carefully. "His passport was Bulgarian."

"Bulgarian?" Beatrice's eyes widened, "the man we are here to investigate is Bulgarian," she lowered her voice. "I don't believe in coincidences."

"Neither do I," Sabine frowned. "Who is the Bulgarian?"

"His name is Ivan Bartzyk; he's called the 'Bulldozer'."

"The 'Bulldozer'?" Sabine sipped her champagne.

"How charming."

"I met Bartzyk last year is Rome; I was working on a story for the Art Digest and arranged to interview him," she paused, a small smile twitching her lips. "Bartzyk is vulgar and crude but still fancies himself quite the ladies man."

"That may work to our advantage."

"May?" Beatrice raised an eyebrow and laughed. "He's a billionaire who has made a fortune in oil and real estate," Beatrice lowered her voice, "and drugs and guns and prostitution. The Company has been unable to pin anything on him; he launders his money through a bank in the Caribbean." Beatrice paused and studied Sabine. "The Company believes Bartzyk is funding Professor Dumere's research," she said slowly. "I understand you know him?"

"I do, and I cannot believe that Professor Dumere…" she stopped under Beatrice's blue gaze. "Well," she inhaled sharply, "there are many questions to be answered."

"Hmm," Beatrice swallowed champagne, "that's true. Tomorrow evening Bartzyk is hosting a cocktail party at his chalet, which we'll be attending."

One step closer to Philippe, Sabine thought,

whatever she had to do.

"The Bulgarian is old school," Beatrice continued, "he has a rabid fear of technology. Bartzyk keeps his files the old-fashioned way—in a wall safe—which may work to our advantage."

"May?" Sabine asked and both women laughed. Sabine relaxed a bit, the warmth of the champagne and Beatrice's company draining the tension from her body. Her instincts told her that Beatrice could be trusted, and that she was as clever and resilient as Sabine. With Beatrice's help this assignment should be successful; dangerous, yes, but both women were experienced and neither of them were fools. "Shall we get a table?" she asked, suddenly ravenous.

"Yes, let's," Beatrice motioned to the bartender, "the fish here is quite good."

"I'm hungry for a steak," Sabine stood up, "very rare."

NINETEEN

"Beatrice! My darling!" Ivan Bartzyk threw open his arms and smothered her in a bear hug. He pulled away, holding her at arm's length, studying her like a farmer contemplating a prize hog. "You look good," he decided, gazing up at her, who towered over his five feet four inch frame, "good enough to eat!" he roared.

Beatrice, in a skin tight gold lame sheath and gold stilettos, smiled sweetly. "Ivan," she squeezed his tree trunk of an arm, "how wonderful to see you again."

The Bulldozer beamed and turned pale gray eyes on Sabine. "And who do we have here?" he demanded.

"This is my cousin Martine from Paris," Beatrice said silkily, "who is visiting me for a week. I told her about your kindness and hospitality, and," she flashed a brilliant smile, "your art collection. You don't mind, do you?"

Ivan Bartzyk stared at Sabine, who was wearing a sleeveless beige shift that fell below her knees, white cotton gloves and thick, black rimmed glasses. "Nyet," he grunted, dismissing Sabine who looked drab next to Beatrice's glittering beauty. "Any cousin of yours is a cousin of mine!" he bellowed, handing them each a glass of champagne. "Come, Beatrice," he slid his arm around her waist, "I want to show you the Manet I just bought—it cost me twenty million euros!" he crowed.

"But Martine…" Beatrice protested feebly as she and Sabine exchanged looks.

"I'll be fine," Sabine murmured.

"She'll be fine," Bartzyk boomed, steering Beatrice in the opposite direction. "See you later, cousin," he called over his shoulder.

Sabine slid through the crowd unnoticed, her dowdy demeanor disappearing amidst the shimmering glamour of The Bulldozer's guests. The women, clad in sumptuous evening gowns bearing haute couture labels and dazzling jewels, mingled with the men, who were wearing impeccably tailored tuxedoes or military uniforms, with an ease of those accustomed to such luxury.

The ballroom in Ivan Bartzyk's chalet was built to resemble a French chateau, with marble floors, gold brocade walls and red velvet draperies hanging from the thirty foot windows. A crystal chandelier hung from the gilt ceiling, shards of light twinkling in the Louis XIV mirrors. A roaring fire crackled in the marble fireplace, its mantle holding two golden candelabrum.

Walking slowly around the opulent room she studied the layout from behind her glasses, pausing at the bottom of the staircase where a red velvet rope hung between the marble pillars blocking the entrance to the second floor.

"Excuse me," she smiled at the sullen guard, who was standing with arms crossed at the bottom of the stairs, "I am an art student from Paris and would love to see the paintings up there," Sabine motioned to the second floor landing. "My classmates at the Conservatory will never believe it when I tell them about all this," she smiled again and adjusted her glasses.

"I am sorry," the guard scowled, "the upstairs is off limits."

"Oh, please," Sabine wheedled, "I'm Beatrice Fontaine's cousin; she is good friends with Mr. Bartzyk."

She saw him hesitate upon mention of Beatrice's name. "I promise I won't touch anything."

The guard stared down at the forlorn figure in the dowdy dress. He knew of The Bulldozer's fondness for Beatrice; what harm could her cousin do? "Very well," he growled, unhooking the rope, "but only for a moment."

"Oh, thank you," Sabine scampered up the stairs.

"And don't go beyond the…"

"I won't," Sabine stopped at the top of the massive staircase and glanced at her wristwatch. She looked down at the guard who was glaring up at her and she waved gaily.

Suddenly an explosion shook the chalet. Shrieks and shouts from the guests reverberated throughout the magnificent room as the guard rushed outside, Sabine forgotten.

Right on time, Sabine thought, racing down the hallway, stopping in front of the third door on the right. Opening her bag she pulled out her lipstick. Turning the tube she aimed the laser at the lock which clicked open.

Inside Bartzyk's office, Sabine adjusted her glasses, the left lens penetrating the walls and scanning the bookcase, the right lens activating the night vision. The room was dominated by a carved oak desk; behind it a black leather chair and ottoman faced the door. A mahogany table ran the length of one wall; the opposite wall was a massive stone fireplace, a bear rug in front of the hearth. He's old school, Sabine thought, where would he keep his safe?

The lens continued scanning as Sabine circled the room, stopping in front of an imposing portrait of Ivan Bartzyk dressed in a military uniform and brandishing a sword. A red light flickered on the lens and Sabine slid a hand under the frame. She pressed a button and the painting swung away from the wall exposing a safe. Sabine pulled the dial panel off and reached into her handbag. Aiming the lipstick tube at the key hole, she twisted the top, the laser clicking open the door.

Sabine spread the folder on the desk and began rifling through the papers. Glancing at her watch she took a deep breath and resumed her search. Suddenly she froze, then lunged under the massive desk as a searchlight outside poured through the windows, its brightness flooding the room. The blinding white beam scanned the area as Sabine held her breath, curled up in a ball under Bartzyk's desk. Slowly, meticulously the searchlight inspected every inch; then, as quickly as it appeared it dissipated, plunging Sabine into darkness once again. In the distance she heard dogs barking and shouting in Bulgarian; Bartzyk's search had moved onward.

She adjusted her glasses, allowing her eyes to grow accustomed to the night vision lenses, and returned to the files on the desk.

She stopped—this was it, the list of his financial empire. Opening her purse, she grabbed her compact and popped off the mirror. Sabine carefully lifted a scanner the size of a postage stamp and began scanning page after page until the file was downloaded.

She replaced the file and closed the door to the safe, returning the portrait to its original position. Silently she crept across the room and slowly opened the door. Glancing in both directions she slunk down the hall in the semi darkness to the staircase.

Suddenly she heard shouting and heavy footsteps running up the stairs. Sabine flattened herself against the wall and held her breath as the men approached.

TWENTY

"More champagne Beatrice?" Ivan Bartzyk, fueled and florid, waved the bottle over Beatrice's half full flute.

"Ivan," Beatrice smiled, "will you join me?"

"Da, da," he bellowed, sloshing champagne into her glass. "So," he gulped from the bottle, "you like my Manet?"

Beatrice stood in front of the masterpiece, her eyes soft. "It is magnificent," she murmured.

"Da," he brayed, "and it cost me twenty million euros."

"You mentioned that," she said lightly.

The Manet was hanging in Bartzyk's private den, an entire wall devoted to its splendor. A brown leather sofa faced it atop a priceless Persian rug. Ten foot candelabras flickered in each corner and the fireplace crackled and sputtered, lending a warm glow to the room.

He gazed up at her, like a two year old in front of a

toy store. "All of this," he waved a stocky arm, "could be yours."

She looked down at him. "Even the Manet?" she teased.

"Of course!" he bellowed, "all of it!"

"Ivan," she demurred, "you're flirting with me."

"Nyet! Nyet!" he roared. "You know how I feel about you. Come, sit down," he grabbed her arm and plopped her onto the sofa. "Beatrice," he fell down beside her, "you are so beautiful," he cooed, stroking her blonde hair, "so beautiful," he lurched forward and enveloped her in a bear hug.

Glancing at her wristwatch as Bartzyk nuzzled her Beatrice frowned. What was Sabine doing? It was…

Suddenly there was a knock on the door. "Go away!" Bartzyk shouted, his face buried in Beatrice's neck.

The knocking continued. "Not now!" he roared.

"Sir," a timid voice called from the hallway, "I am sorry to disturb you, but this is important."

Cursing in Bulgarian, Bartzyk stormed across the room. "What?" he demanded, flinging open the door.

Standing in the hallway were two sheepish looking guards and Sabine, blinking big eyes from behind her glasses.

"Sir," a guard handed Bartzyk Sabine's purse, "we found her napping in the library."

"In the library?" Bartzyk asked softly, studying Sabine. He opened her purse, which contained a lipstick and a compact. "Napping in the library?" he snapped the purse shut, his eyes narrow.

"Martine, I am so sorry," Beatrice gushed, gliding across the room. "Ivan," she clutched Sabine's hand and turned to Bartzyk, "you remember my cousin?" She turned back to Sabine. "Please forgive me. Ivan was showing me his art collection and I lost track of time. It is breathtaking."

"I know," Sabine chirped, "the guard was nice enough to let me view the exhibit at the top of the stairs, and suddenly I felt dizzy and had to sit down. The door was open," she paused for a breath, "I must have dozed off."

"Poor darling," Beatrice stroked her arm, "it was such a long trip from Paris today."

"And I'm not used to drinking champagne," Sabine blinked big eyes.

"Ivan," Beatrice cooed, "this is all my fault. Please forgive me, won't you?" she flashed a dazzling smile.

Bartzyk studied the two women, his face hard, then

he shrugged, shoving the purse in Sabine's direction. "Of course, of course, no harm done. Let's have another glass of champagne."

"As much as I would love to," Beatrice purred, "I must take Martine home—I'm afraid I've neglected her. Tomorrow?" she smiled, "lunch?"

"I prefer dinner," Bartzyk growled, "da, da," he turned to the guards, "bring Madame's car around. Ladies," he bowed stiffly, "good evening."

Stepping out into the cold night air both women took deep breaths. "Well," Beatrice slid behind the steering wheel, "that was too close for comfort."

"For me or for you?"

Beatrice laughed shortly. "For both of us," she sped down the winding mountain road, glancing in the rear view mirror. "Were you successful?"

"Da," Sabine took off her glasses, "your dear friend has quite the financial organization." She checked the side view mirror. "No doubt he'll demand a pre-nup."

"No doubt," Beatrice said dryly. "Not used to drinking champagne?" She threw Sabine a side long glance. "I nearly burst into laughter."

"I'm not used to drinking champagne," Sabine said slowly, "in such small quantities."

TWENTY ONE

A persistent knocking on the door stirred Sabine from her slumber. Opening one eye she called, "who is it?"

"Beatrice."

"Beatrice," she sat up and wrapped the duvet around her naked body, "come in; the door is unlocked."

Beatrice, in black ski pants and a royal blue turtleneck sweater, pushed open the adjoining door to the bedroom carrying a silver tray. "Good morning," she said briskly, placing the tray on the foot of Sabine's bed, "even if it is nearly noon."

"Noon?" Sabine ran a hand through her short hair, "no!"

"Yes," Beatrice smiled and pulled up a chair. "I've been up since six."

Sabine stifled a shudder. "I've never been a morning person."

"Obviously; I took the liberty of ordering breakfast. Our plane leaves at four."

"Our plane?" Sabine blinked. "Where are we going?"

Beatrice poured coffee into a porcelain cup. "Cream? Sugar?"

Sabine nodded, still staring at Beatrice.

"I spoke to Gruber this morning," Beatrice handed Sabine her coffee, "the information we sent them last night confirms their suspicions; Bartzyk is laundering money through the Cayman Islands to a bank in the Bahamas where it is clean."

Sabine ripped apart a croissant. "What happens in the Bahamas?"

"The funds are then deposited to a foundation in the Florida Keys; Key Largo, specifically."

"Are these deposits and withdrawals done electronically?"

"Sometimes," Beatrice said slowly, "sometimes the funds are withdrawn in person."

"Does the bank in Freeport have security records of these transactions?"

Beatrice shook her head. "No, no cameras, which has made following the money even more difficult."

"Does the Company know what sort of foundation it is?"

"The Company can't find it; layers and layers of shell companies are hiding it. The Company believes it is necessary to catch the conspirators with their hands in the cookie jar, so to speak." Beatrice paused, "that's why you're flying to Freeport tonight."

"Tonight?" Sabine swallowed coffee. "I? Not we?"

Beatrice smiled. "The plane is dropping me off in Paris before taking you to Freeport."

"Too bad," Sabine murmured.

"Yes," Beatrice sipped her coffee.

"So," Sabine smiled, "no lunch with the Bulldozer?"

Beatrice laughed shortly. "No lunch, no dinner. The Company feels it is best to put some space between us." She paused. "Since Bartzyk knows me if I were to show up in Freeport it would jeopardize the investigation." She paused again. "I dare say you won't be recognized as my cousin Martine."

Sabine grimaced. "I hope not."

"The British have promised their cooperation but…"

"But?"

"At a discreet distance."

Sabine laughed shortly. "How discreet of them."

"Mmmm," Beatrice's expression was serious, "it appears you are on your own for this one."

Sabine frowned. "This plan sounds tenuous, at best." Working solitary on a dangerous assignment, a confrontation with the mastermind of the money laundering scheme a distinct possibility…Sabine bit her bottom lip; her instincts told her that it was too risky, even for an agent with her experience. Then Philippe's face swam before her, his eyes soft, beckoning her. One step closer, she inhaled sharply; whatever she had to do.

"Well," Sabine glanced outside at the snow covered roofs of the chalets, "I love the ocean, and I'm sure the Company will have a new wardrobe waiting for me," she stopped. "At least it will be warm."

"Let's hope," Beatrice paused, her face grim, "not too warm."

TWENTY TWO

Ivan Bartzyk stood at the double windows in the study of his chalet, staring out at the snow capped mountains, the bright blue sky painting a vivid backdrop in the late morning sunshine. He glanced down at the town below, the people bustling in the cold air to and fro as energetic as ants. Stifling a shudder, he walked to the table and poured himself a cognac, unable to rid himself of the chill in his bones. He rubbed his left leg, the frigid temperatures tightening his muscles. For a moment he was back in the Siberian labor camp, always cold, always hungry. Ten years, he gulped cognac, he had languished in the frozen void, but had survived the prison and the man who had nearly severed his leg. He silently praised his instincts that had kept him alive where so many others died. Bartzyk stared up at his portrait, his mouth full of cognac—again his instincts whispered to him that something was not right, but what was it?

The explosion last night revealed nothing was stolen; still, his gut told him something was wrong. Something was wrong, he banged his desk with his fist, what? what?

The telephone on his desk rang, disrupting his concentration. "What do you want?" he bellowed into the receiver.

"Sir, there is a call for you, a Miss Fontaine."

"Of course," he grunted, "put it through." He swallowed cognac. "Beatrice, my darling," he cooed, "I was just thinking of you…it is true…I was thinking that I hoped you and your cousin enjoyed my little party last night…I'm glad…yes…you're very kind…so, my darling, are we meeting for lunch today?" He frowned. "Of course," he said softly, "yes, I understand completely…another time then…give my best to your cousin," he paused, "I hope to see both of you very soon."

Bartzyk hung up the receiver, the gnawing in his stomach more violent. He continued staring at his portrait, his pale eyes narrow.

The study door opened slightly after a timid knock. "I told you I did not want to be disturbed!" he roared.

"I am sorry to interrupt Sir, but there is good news that I believe you would want to hear."

Bartzyk stared at him. "Really?" he sneered. "I could use some good news right now. What is it?"

"Sir," he stammered, adjusting his glasses, "Torin Bataar…"

"Torin Bataar?" Bartzyk whispered, his face ashen. "What about him?"

"Sir, he's been…"

"Killed?"

"Captured."

"Captured? Where?"

"Inner Mongolia, not far from the border."

"By whom?" Bartzyk narrowed his eyes. "The Russians?"

"No, sir, the Chinese."

"The Chinese," Bartzyk muttered, "even better."

"Bataar is being held at a maximum security prison outside of Hohhot."

"Torin Bataar in a Chinese prison," Bartzyk murmured, "so the Scorpion has been caged. This day has improved." He swallowed cognac and walked to the table. "Leave me," he commanded.

Bartzyk filled his crystal glass and eased himself

into his leather chair. Lifting his left leg with his two hands he propped it onto the black leather ottoman and exhaled slowly. "So, my old friend," he whispered, "your luck has changed, and perhaps mine will, too."

The telephone rang again. "Yes?"

"Sir, there is a call for you but the gentleman won't give his name."

"Won't give his name?" he roared.

"No, Sir, but he insists that he must speak with you. He's calling from Paris."

"Paris?" Bartzyk muttered, "put him through on the secure line."

Bartzyk reached for the cigar box. "Yes, yes…I have just received good news—I hope you are calling with more…you are?" Bartzyk bit off the end of the cigar and spat it on the floor. "So you heard from our friend in the tropics?" Bartzyk lit his cigar and exhaled smoke. "Yes," his eyes widened, "that is good news…of course, as usual…ciao."

Bartzyk replaced the receiver, smiling; first the capture of Torin Bataar and now…he picked up the telephone. "Tell the pilot to prepare my jet," he swallowed a mouthful of cognac, "we are leaving soon for a warmer climate."

TWENTY THREE

Sabine stood on the white latticed terrace of her hotel suite and stared at the panorama before her. Past the vivid green lawn and palm trees the white sand beach sparkled like tiny diamonds in the mid morning sunshine, the turquoise ocean gently lapping the shore. A lone sailboat, its yellow sail luffing in the breeze, headed out into the sea of blue. Above, white billows of clouds dotted the cerulean sky. Yesterday I was staring at mountains, she mused, breathing in the briny air and unwrapping the towel from her damp hair and tossing it onto the white rattan chair.

She had arrived in Freeport last evening, the Company plane landing at a private air field, and was driven to the beach front hotel. As she predicted, a new wardrobe was waiting for her, suitable for the tropical climate. Sabine turned and looked at the spacious bedroom—the Company spared no expense for this assignment. The white marble floor reflected the light pouring in from the balcony. Against the lavender walls the massive mahogany head board of the king size bed gleamed with glints of red in the sun. At the foot of the bed a lavender brocade bench, bedecked with silk pillows, nestled against the lilac satin duvet. Off the bedroom the coral sitting room was furnished with a white settee and chairs; against one wall a dark wood table was stocked with Sabine's favorite brand of bourbon.

The Company thinks of everything, Sabine decided, compensation for a dangerous assignment. She laughed shortly; perhaps the Company wanted what could be her final operation to be as pleasant as possible. Sabine frowned, glancing at the clock atop the white rattan table; nearly ten thirty—breakfast will be arriving soon, and then off to Bartzyk's bank… she needed to be as focused and careful as possible.

An energetic knock on the door caused her to jump. Slipping the .22 into the pocket of her robe she walked to the door. "Who is it?"

"Room service, Madame."

Sabine unlocked the door; there stood a smiling waiter in a crisp jacket. "Good morning. Would

Madame like breakfast on the terrace?"

"Yes, thank you."

"Very good," he wheeled the cart into the sunshine and picked up the towel she had thrown onto the chair. "Enjoy your day, Madame."

Sabine poured coffee into a cup and stared at the vast blue expanse. "Enjoy my day," she murmured; the past weeks had culminated into what could be a fatal confrontation with Bartzyk's thugs—ruthless and relentless and willing to kill or be killed. And what of Philippe and his uncle? It wasn't possible that they were involved, was it? Sabine continued gazing at the blue sea before her, but her thoughts were a million miles away. "Enjoy my day," she repeated, her face grim.

Two hours later Sabine, in a sun dress and straw hat, was strolling the cobblestone streets of Freeport ambling her way through the neighborhood where Bartzyk's bank was located, a miniscule camera imbedded in her sunglasses recording every detail. Past the vivid blue and pink buildings, trimmed in white and festooned with colorful flower boxes, she saw the building ten meters ahead. She stopped to admire a table of hand woven straw bags, gazing at the bank from behind the dark lenses. She smiled and continued walking until the pink bank was directly ahead. A small cafe with two outside tables was across the street; perfect, Sabine thought.

Sitting down on a white metal chair Sabine studied the structure; single story, one front door, two windows, probably one back exit. Sabine opened her bag and removed her cell phone, forwarding the images recorded to the Company's surveillance center.

A waiter approached the table. "Would Madame like to see a menu?"

Sabine glanced away from the bank and smiled up at the waiter. "Yes, please, and a glass of white…" she paused and froze.

Walking out of the front door of the bank was a dark haired man with a beard and a familiar gait. He looked both ways before he snapped on his black helmet and tossed a long leg over his red motorcycle. Revving the engine he roared off as Sabine stood up.

The man was Philippe.

TWENTY FOUR

"I've changed my mind—I must go!" Sabine glanced at the waiter's startled face. "Forgive me; another time perhaps. Taxi!" She ran into the street, one arm raised. A cab screeched to a stop and she flung open the back door. "That red motorcycle ahead—follow him!"

"Very good, Madame," the driver sped off in the direction of Philippe's retreating form. Sabine, perched on the edge of the back seat, tore off her sunglasses and scanned the road ahead. "There!" she cried. "I see him!"

"As do I, Madame," the driver murmured as he shifted gears, the taxi shaking and rumbling.

The driver careened through the narrow streets of Freeport at a break neck speed, his gaze fixed on Philippe's motorcycle like a hunting dog. The vibrant colors whizzed by in a blur as Sabine lurched to and fro in the lumpy back seat. Tearing off her straw hat she craned her neck. "Where is he?" she demanded.

The driver glanced at her in the rear view mirror. "Madame, he just turned the corner."

"Don't lose him!"

Sabine dug her nails into the black upholstery as the taxi careened around the corner and sped off after Philippe, who was a blur of red in the distance. Red, Sabine thought, like the man in the red jacket that I chased through the Luxembourg Gardens. Could she be mistaken again? No, she whispered, this time I'm sure it's him.

Sabine leaned forward on the seat, scanning the road ahead. "I don't see him."

"But I do, Madame," the driver said calmly. "He is just ahead; please do not worry."

Suddenly a flower cart pulled out into the street and the driver slammed on the brakes. Cursing and shouting, the driver waved the elderly woman to the side and screeched off in the direction of Philippe, who was heading out of the center of the city towards the waterfront.

"Where has he gone?" Sabine cried.

"He is heading for the docks." The driver studied Sabine's anguished face from the rear view mirror.

"I know this city well, Madame; there are only a few streets that lead to the ocean."

"Please, Sabine begged, "whatever you do, don't lose him!"

Twenty minutes later, after an exhaustive search of the narrow cobblestone paths of the neighborhood, the driver pulled over and stopped the taxi. "Madame, I am sorry; he has disappeared."

"He has a habit of doing that," Sabine said bitterly.

"Does Madame wish me to resume the search?"

Sabine shook her head. "No, I'm going to get out and walk for a bit." She handed him a one hundred dollar bill. "Thank you."

He gazed at the bill, his eyes wide. "It seems that Madame wanted very much to catch that man."

"Very much," Sabine murmured, slamming the door shut.

She stumbled through the crowded streets of the waterfront, her mind racing. The sun was hot on her face, her straw hat and sunglasses left in the back seat of the taxi. Philippe…working for Bartzyk? Sabine felt as if she'd been kicked in the stomach. All this time, could she have been wrong about Philippe? Was he a traitor? Was he the person Pascal warned her not to trust? Did Philippe murder him because Pascal knew his secret? She staggered along the cobblestone street, choking back tears; Philippe, the man she cherished, had he gone rogue?

No, no, she grit her teeth, there had to be another explanation; if she could see him, talk to him. Think…think, she whispered savagely, where was he? She knew him…where would he go?

Sabine turned a corner and a cool breeze embraced her. She could see the ocean, the smell of sea air filling her lungs, the cries of seagulls shrill and piercing. Instinctively she headed towards the water where the sailboats bobbed up and down like tops in the gentle waves.

She walked down the wooden dock, glancing from side to side at the boats. Her heart racing, her throat dry, she came to the end of the pier. There, flying a French flag atop the mainmast, was a thirty foot sailboat. On the port side, painted in red, 'Sabine II'.

TWENTY FIVE

"Philippe?"

The man turned. There he stood, in the galley of the sailboat, barefoot and bare chested, holding a glass of white wine. His sun tanned face split into a smile until he saw the gun pointed at him.

"Welcome aboard Madame," he sipped his wine, "have you come for dinner or to shoot me? As you can see, I have been shot before," he waved his hand across his chest where the scars of two bullet holes remained, "so I do hope you are here to dine with me." He studied her, his brown eyes glittering. "If so, please lower your weapon; it is making the chef nervous." He smiled again. "Would you like a glass of wine? It is your favorite, from the Loire." He gazed at her, his eyes soft. "I like your haircut; it is very chic."

Sabine continued pointing her gun at him, her breath rapid. "Philippe…"

"Sabine," he poured wine into a glass, "how can you shoot me," he held it out to her, "when you are drinking this?"

She frowned. "I am an excellent shot," she said coolly.

Philippe laughed. "You are the best, but you will not enjoy this wine if you are thinking about shooting me," he smiled. "I promise I will not try to escape."

Sabine lowered her gun slowly. "As long as I have your word," she said sarcastically, reaching for the glass.

Philippe laughed again. "So," he gestured with his arm, "how do you like my chateau? It is not as cozy as the first, but I make do." He turned to her, his eyes tender. "As you can see it could use a woman's touch."

Past the mahogany bar of the galley the boat was furnished with the bare necessities. A white rattan settee and chairs encircled a low wooden table in the living area. Sheer white curtains hung across the doorway to the sleeping alcove in the bow. She glanced at a picture in a gold frame on a wicker table and caught her breath; it was she, Philippe and his uncle Stephane the summer they spent at the Cote d'Azur. All three were laughing into the camera, the turquoise sea behind them.

He followed her gaze. "The Company was thoughtful enough to salvage a few of my personal belongings from the 'Sabine I'."

She swallowed wine and glanced at Philippe, whose expression was inscrutable. "It is very…comfortable."

"Thank you, Madame," he bowed slightly, "and now, I shall resume my dinner preparations." He smiled at her. "I do hope you will join me; these past months I have grown accustomed to dining alone, which is not always enjoyable. Our dinners together were always," Philippe paused, studying her, "very enjoyable. I have enough food for two."

"Were you expecting someone?"

Philippe shrugged. "I knew I was being followed, and that the taxi would lose me. If I had known it was you," he grinned, "I would have slowed down."

"How kind you are," she snapped, suddenly furious. His lies, his deception, his charade that had made her life a living hell, and now, to see him again, with questions that needed answers, and to be met with his arrogance…after the past months of heartache and loss Philippe's nonchalance enraged her. "What sort of a game are you playing?"

"Game?" he murmured, his head low. "It is not a game when I am cooking, especially your favorite… red snapper." He straightened and looked at her anguished face. "Cherie," he said softly, "it was never a game between us."

"Philippe…" she choked back a sob.

And then she was in his arms, his kisses wet from her tears. "Philippe," she murmured, "what…"

He put a finger to her lips. "Later."

TWENTY SIX

Waves were rocking the boat gently back and forth; she was in an unfamiliar place but Philippe was there. She was sitting at a wooden table with a white tablecloth looking up at him. He was smiling down at her, pouring red wine into a glass. She laughed and suddenly the boat lurched, spilling the wine. Red wine soaked the white linen as the boat rocked violently. The wine turned into blood; blood was everywhere. Sabine gasped for air; she was underwater in darkness; suddenly an explosion propelled her up and out of the water.

She sat up in bed, soaked in sweat, and reached for her gun. "Philippe?" she asked hesitantly.

He popped his head out of the bathroom, his face covered in shaving cream, and smiled. "Good morning, Madame, or should I say good afternoon?"

She stared at him; he was wearing just a towel, his

dark hair damp from the shower. She wasn't dreaming—Philippe was real.

He stared back. "Are you going to shoot me?"

"No," she smiled and relaxed against the pillows, "as long as you are shaving that beard, and you bring me coffee."

"Yes, yes, Madame. May I wash my face first?"

Sabine laughed. "Yes, but hurry."

He strode into the galley, his tanned body gleaming against the white towel. She glanced at the scars on his chest from the bullets than nearly killed him and stifled a shudder.

"Madame," he sat down on the bed, "your coffee, the way you like it; cream and one sugar."

"How do you know that's still how I like it?" she teased.

"Because," he stroked her arm, "I know you, body and soul."

"Philippe, why didn't you tell me you were alive?"

"Sabine," his voice was tender, "I couldn't; I was already a target. It would have endangered you." He gazed at her, his brown eyes soft. "I would do anything to keep you safe."

Sabine swallowed hard. "I wanted to die when I

thought you were gone."

"I am very glad you didn't," he announced, his mood suddenly light, "because," his hand dove under the sheet and grabbed her leg, "I am very attached to this little foot."

She laughed and pushed him away. "Not as attached as I am. Philippe," she said softly, "do you have your knife?"

"My knife?" he blinked. "No, it was on the boat in Paris. Why?"

She inhaled sharply. "There's a reason why I'm here."

"Yes?" his eyes glittered. "Was it last night or this morning?"

"Oh, la la," she frowned, "perhaps I will shoot you after all."

He laughed and fell on top of her, wrapping his arms around her naked body. "Sabine," he kissed her neck, "I am just glad that you found me."

She put a hand on his chest. "But it wasn't an accident; the Company…" she stopped.

"The Company?" he sat up, his face grim. "Why are they involved?"

"Because," she bit her bottom lip, "they believe

your uncle is planning an attack."

"Uncle Stephane?" Philippe blinked. "But that is ridiculous!" he stood up. "He is a research scientist, not a terrorist!" his voice rose. He paused and looked down at her. "What sort of attack?"

"The Company doesn't know; the operation is being financed by Ivan Bartzyk."

"Bartzyk?" Philippe frowned. "The Bulgarian? No, no," he shook his head and paced across the room, "Uncle Stephane doesn't even know him, much less work for him."

"Philippe, the man who shot you," she swallowed, "he was Bulgarian."

"Was?" Philippe stared at her. "How do you know?"

"Because I killed him."

Philippe continued staring at her angry, anguished face. "Cherie," he said softly, "I'm sorry…"

"I'm not," she snapped, "besides, he was trying to kill me."

Philippe sat down on the bed and stroked her hand. "Sabine…"

She threw her arms around his neck and buried her face in his shoulder. "You don't know how horrible it was, when I thought you were dead…"

"Mon coeur," he murmured, wiping her tears, "forgive me." He stroked her hair. "So both Bartzyk and the man you shot are Bulgarian—how does that implicate Uncle Stephane?"

"Philippe, the bank you were at yesterday, Ivan Bartzyk owns it. He launders money through the Cayman Islands to Freeport." She paused. "Why were you there?"

"Because of the Foundation that is funding Uncle Stephane's research," he said slowly, "their account is there; I withdrew money for him." He paused and shook his head again. "No, I cannot believe it; it must be a mistake." He stared at her, his face hard. "So that is why you are here? To investigate Uncle Stephane?"

Sabine nodded. "I told the Chairman they were wrong, that neither of you could be involved."

Philippe smiled slyly. "The Company thinks I'm involved?"

"Yes," she said softly, "they were…irritated that you gave them the slip after you were shot."

Philippe laughed shortly. "I'm sure they were. The Company did not do a very good job of protecting me so I disappeared; I was safer without their help." He fixed his gaze on her. "Did you ever think we were involved?"

She shook her head. "Not for one second did I believe it."

"Madame," he put his hand on his heart, "I am touched by your faith in me, and, after lunch, I shall endeavor to make good on your trust."

"How?"

"We will set sail for the Florida Keys where Uncle Stephane is conducting his scientific research. I shall clear the good name of the Dumere family and honor will be restored. I will prove our innocence once and for all."

Philippe raised one hand, the other hand over his heart, a silly expression on his face and Sabine caught her breath. The months of sadness and sorrow without him came rushing back, squeezing the air from her lungs. She stared at him, an ache filling her soul. I'm not dreaming, she thought, he is real, I found him…

Sabine grabbed him around the neck and pulled him down on the bed. "You can restore your family honor," she tore off his towel, "tomorrow."

TWENTY SEVEN

"A coffee, please?"

Heinrich Gruber slid into the black banquette and studied his reflection in the mirror across the room. It was mid afternoon and half of the marble topped tables in the Paris cafe were full, people lingering over coffee and reading newspapers. The sun streamed in through the front windows, the zinc topped mahogany bar glinting maroon in the light. The waitress approached with his coffee and he smoothed his hair. "Merci," he smiled up at her, and she smiled back. "Would Monsieur like to see a menu?"

Gruber looked her up and down as a slow flush colored her cheeks. "I don't need a menu," he grinned, "I am sure of what I want."

"Bien," she murmured, "I will be right with Monsieur," she walked away quickly, her brow furrowed in a frown.

He glanced around the cafe and snapped open his cell phone. "Good afternoon, this is Heinrich Gruber calling to speak to the Chairman...of course I will hold...hello, sir...yes, she has made contact with our friend...yesterday afternoon...and this morning, no doubt," he snorted. "Yes, of course," Gruber cleared his throat, "forgive me...he's living on a sailboat in the Bahamas...one of our men picked her up in a taxi and dropped her near the docks...the video surveillance was interrupted but the driver is sending us regular reports... yes, sir, your instincts were correct—only she could have found him," he sipped his coffee. "We can track both of them through her cell phone...yes, sir, the plan is working...just a few more loose ends...yes, sir, only a matter of time... very good...ciao."

Gruber motioned to the waitress for his check as he studied himself in the mirror. She approached the table, her eyes lowered, and dropped the bill. "Merci, Madame," he called after her retreating figure. Scribbling his telephone number on the receipt, he smiled; perhaps she was one of those women who enjoys playing hard to get. The thought cheered him as he stepped out into the late afternoon sun and adjusted his scarf. An attractive blonde woman wearing a red beret walked to the cafe door; Gruber caught her eye and smiled. "Would you like to join me for a coffee?" Gruber glanced at his reflection in the cafe window. "Let's go around the corner—the service here is very bad."

TWENTY EIGHT

Aquarius, an undersea laboratory dedicated solely to marine science, was the only facility of its kind in the world. The 82 ton habitat, deployed on the ocean floor sixty feet below sea level, in addition to its scientific facilities, housed living quarters, enabling scientists to use saturation diving to study and explore the sea. Located on Conch Reef three miles offshore and nine miles from Key Largo, Aquarius was attached to a base plate that positioned the underwater lab. Moored above, the Life Support Buoy supplied the oxygen, power and communication systems necessary for the scientists' survival. An umbilical cord of cables connecting the Buoy to Aquarius allowed them to live and work underwater.

Over the past fifty years Aquarius had hosted a number of illustrious scientists but none more brilliant and respected as Professor Stephane Dumere from the Sorbonne. For the past three months he had been conducting experiments involving the release of methane into the earth's atmosphere and its consequences. Decades of research had culminated in his work twenty meters below the sea, where he and his assistants were staging carefully controlled experiments in the fragile ecosystem of the Florida Keys. The project, funded by an anonymous foundation familiar with Professor Dumere's expertise, was shrouded in secrecy, with the scientists being told only the necessary information to conduct their work. Professor Dumere monitored the progress from the Mission Control Center at Key Largo, located on a remote part of the island. A private air strip and dock enabled the team to move about in secrecy, away from public scrutiny.

The day had dawned brilliant and clear in the Keys. A languid breeze rustled the palm fronds and the smell of hibiscus perfumed the warm air. The sun shone brightly in the cloudless sky, as blue as the sea below.

    Professor Dumere walked across the landscaped grounds from his private bungalow to the Mission Control Center, his brow furrowed. He had spent the morning studying the data from last week's diving expedition and was waiting anxiously for this week's results.

Professor Dumere punched in his security code and the heavy door to Mission Control clicked open. He walked into the laboratory where a dozen computers were monitoring Aquarius via wireless telemetry. A young man, in a white lab coat and thick, black rimmed glasses, tore his gaze away from the screens as Professor Dumere approached.

"Good afternoon, Professor."

"Hello, Lucien," he smiled, his eyes tired. "Have you had your lunch yet?"

"No, sir; I was waiting for the data from this week's dive."

The Professor pulled out a chair. "You mustn't go hungry—the report should be coming in very soon." His expression brightened. "I heard from my nephew; he should be arriving later this afternoon, and he's bringing a guest."

"A guest?" Lucien, frowning, adjusted his black rimmed glasses. "Beg pardon, Professor, but is that wise?"

"She's like a daughter to me; I trust her with my life."

Lucien turned back to the computer. "The data from the last experiment is here Professor."

Professor Dumere studied the screen, his face turning white. "So it's true; my hypothesis was proven correct," he whispered, "for once I wish I had been wrong."

Lucien stared at the Professor's ashen face, "Professor, what is it?"

Professor Dumere swallowed hard. "What caused the mass extinction at the end of the Triassic period can be engineered," he paused, "with horrific results. It could produce a weapon of such magnitude...my God," he put his head in his hands, "what have I done?"

"Professor," Lucien was gazing at the security camera monitoring the outside perimeter, "you'd better take a look at this."

TWENTY NINE

"The Gulf Stream was with us."

Philippe, at the helm of the 'Sabine II', turned and smiled at Sabine, who was sitting port side. "We are approaching Key Largo. The Aquarius lab is only a few miles away." He paused, gazing at her, who smiled back. "Madame," he said with mock severity, " this is not a pleasure cruise. Haul in the jib; it is luffing."

"Yes, sir," Sabine murmured, tugging on the line. "Forgive my inattentiveness."

"You are forgiven," Philippe declared. "No doubt you were contemplating my excellent seamanship."

"No doubt," Sabine said dryly, trying not to smile.

"Or perhaps you were studying my," he paused and turned to her, a sly smile on his sun tanned face, "exquisite form?"

"Your exquisite form?" Sabine murmured. "Monsieur…"

"Madame," Philippe held up one hand, "address me as 'Captain' or 'Sir' aboard this vessel."

"Captain Sir," Sabine pursed her lips, "do not forget that I am an experienced sailor also; if you should accidentally fall into the ocean I am perfectly capable of commanding the helm."

"You would not declare 'man overboard'?" he cried in mock horror. "What you suggest, Madame, is mutiny."

"No Captain Sir," Sabine said slowly, "it is mercy killing."

Philippe threw back his head and laughed as Sabine stared at his profile outlined against the horizon. The past days with Philippe had settled into a familiar intimacy, as if their time apart had been hours instead of months. Neither of them spoke again of the reason for their voyage, or the weeks without each other; what was important was that they were together again, each content with the other, each trusting the other.

Sabine continued gazing at him, his handsome profile etched against the early evening sky, committing to memory every detail of him, compensating for her months without him, an inconsolable emptiness that had consumed her like an insatiable hunger. She inhaled deeply, the smell of Philippe still lingering on her body and she smiled, remembering last night.

They had set sail at first light and had been blessed with calm seas and a steady wind. At mid day a pod of dolphins had swum alongside for several miles, frolicking and playing in the aqua ocean. Now the sun had begun its descent, tinting the cerulean sky with wisps of pink.

"What do you think of the 'Sabine II'?" Philippe asked.

"Well, Captain Sir, you must realize that I still have a soft spot for the 'Sabine I'." She paused, her gaze still fixed on Philippe. "What happened to her?" she asked softly.

Philippe shrugged, his face inscrutable. "The Company had it towed when I was in the hospital." He was silent for a moment. "But the 'Sabine II' is yar; we have made excellent time," he paused, his mood cheerful again. "We are very close to 'Aquarius'."

"Excellent time?" Sabine widened her eyes. "Captain Sir, we have been sailing for nearly eleven hours; you woke me up at the crack of dawn."

"As I remember," Philippe glanced in her direction,

"you were not asleep."

Sabine laughed. "I was not allowed to sleep."

"Madame, my intentions were honorable, I assure you! I kept you awake all night because I feared the months you lived in the country had made you lazy!"

"Lazy?" Sabine murmured, smiling. "Gruber accused me of being lazy when we were in Paris."

"Gruber?" Philippe frowned. "I don't like that man, and I don't trust him."

"The only man I trust," Sabine said slowly, "is you."

"Thank you Madame," Philippe smiled. "It is true, I did keep you awake all night, but," he gestured with one hand, "look at what you might have missed."

"What I might have missed," Sabine whispered.

The sun was setting in the Florida Keys, a vivid ball of fire descending in the distance, painting the sky in streaks of orange and red. Pink hued clouds billowed up against the horizon like far away mountains. Turquoise waves rocked the sailboat gently, the smell of the sea perfuming the air. A solitary sea gull swooped and shrieked, its mournful cry shattering the silence.

"Oh, darling," she cried, suddenly overwhelmed, "can't we just go on sailing and forget about plots and secret agencies? Can't we just disappear together?"

Philippe studied her, his eyes soft. "Is that what you would like to do, cherie?"

"Oh, yes," she stood up and wrapped her arms around his waist, "more than anything."

"Your offer is very tempting," Philippe smiled, his mood light, "but I have already contacted Uncle Stephane; no doubt he has a delicious dinner waiting for us. His cooking is not as brilliant as mine; still, it would be bad manners to sail off into the sunset."

"Oh la la," Sabine murmured, rubbing her face against his arm, "you were not so concerned with good manners last night."

Philippe laughed and scanned the horizon. "I see the Life Support Buoy," he pointed to a bright light atop a yellow metal spire in the distance. "We are very close to the lab." He continued staring, his smile disappearing. "That is strange," he murmured. "Hand me the binoculars, Sabine."

Sabine scanned his face in the waning light. "Philippe, what is it?"

"I'm not sure," Philippe said slowly, staring through the lenses. "I am heading for the buoy."

Ten minutes later Philippe pulled up along side the Buoy. "Ahoy," he called. "Uncle Stephane! What are you doing out here this time of night?"

Professor Dumere shook his head slowly. "My boy," he whispered, "I am so sorry."

"Sorry?" Philippe cried. "Why are you…" he stopped. From out of the shadows a man walked into the floodlight.

The man was Ivan Bartzyk.

THIRTY

"Permission to come aboard?" Bartzyk roared, standing next to Professor Dumere atop the Life Support Buoy. He motioned to his two men who leveled their guns at Philippe and Sabine. Bartzyk hoisted his bulky frame over the side of the buoy and onto the deck of the sailboat, his beefy face flushed from the exertion. "Miss Jouey, or should I say 'Martine'?" he leered, wiping his forehead, "I almost didn't recognize you without your glasses. And Philippe, what a pleasant surprise to see both of you."

"Why are you here?" Philippe demanded. "What is all this about?"

"This is about," Bartzyk nodded in the direction of Professor Dumere, "him. Your uncle is refusing to turn over the results of his research that my foundation funded."

"But I didn't know that!" Professor Dumere cried.

"I didn't know it was your money! If I had I never would have agreed to it!"

"Minor details," Bartzyk murmured. "You did and now I want what I paid for." He smiled at Philippe. "Months ago I set up a foundation for your uncle to continue his research on his theories of extinction. I asked no questions and gave him everything he wanted. I have been most generous, but now I am here to collect the data that is mine. Since your uncle was reluctant to comply with my request, I thought a visit to the Buoy with the prospect of cutting off the life support to his men below would..." he paused, "inspire him to reconsider. Your arrival was an unexpected stroke of luck."

"Luck?" Philippe spat. "What kind of a man are you?"

"I am a businessman," Bartzyk said calmly. "If I possessed this research I would be the most powerful man in the world."

"Philippe," Professor Dumere shouted, "my work could be corrupted into a terrible weapon, capable of destroying all life on earth. You understand why I cannot turn it over to him."

"I do understand," Philippe muttered. "Under no

circumstances can that happen."

"It seems we have reached a stalemate," Bartzyk reached into his jacket pocket and pulled out a gun. "On your knees, hands on your heads, both of you."

Philippe and Sabine knelt slowly in front of him as he paced back and forth. "So, Professor," he called over his shoulder, "who is it to be? Philippe? You have proven to be a difficult man to kill, but as the saying goes 'if you want something done…'" he turned to Sabine. "Or the beautiful Miss Jouey?" he paused and placed the barrel of the gun in the middle of her forehead. "What a pity to destroy such an exquisite face," he murmured. "Perhaps you would like to," he slid the gun slowly down her neck, resting the barrel between her breasts, "go below and beg me for mercy?"

"She has nothing to do with this!" Philippe roared.

"On the contrary," Bartzyk smiled, stroking Sabine's hair. "The Professor loves her like a daughter. I saw a picture he has of the three of you in his laboratory. "So you see," he turned back to Sabine, "she is as involved as both of you."

"You are a coward," Philippe sneered, "to threaten an unarmed woman."

"She may be unarmed, but she is hardly helpless.

She killed one of my best operatives." He turned to Philippe. "But it is heartwarming to see that chivalry is not dead. I have heard of the gallant French men but I am not French and not bound by such rules. So Miss Jouey," he cupped her face in his hand, "are you ready to plead for your life?"

Sabine looked up at Bartzyk and smiled, rubbing her face against his palm. Suddenly she opened her mouth and bit him savagely on the hand, blood spurting from his torn flesh.

Bartzky roared as Sabine continued to bite down. He shook her off and slapped her viciously, sending her sprawling across the deck. "I will enjoy this," he declared, his pale eyes glittering as he pointed the gun at her head.

"NO!" Philippe shouted, standing up as Bartzyk's men leveled both guns at him. "No," he murmured, bending over Sabine. "Are you hurt, cherie?"

Sabine moaned, her face throbbing with pain.

Philippe turned to Bartzyk. "Kill me, but give me your word you will not harm her."

"I give you my word," Bartzyk growled, aiming the gun at Philippe, "that I will kill you first."

THIRTY ONE

Sabine stared up at the night sky; the full moon was shimmering on the calm seas, the stars glittering like diamonds on dark blue velvet. She was being rocked gently, the waves rhythmically lapping the sides of the boat. Philippe was there—he was standing over her, speaking to her but she couldn't hear him. Ringing, Sabine closed her eyes; she heard ringing, faintly at first and then louder—the bell atop the Life Support Buoy was clanging a death knell.

She opened her eyes; she heard shouting—voices she didn't recognize, voices with heavy accents, and Philippe, she heard Philippe shouting, like that night in Paris months ago, on the 'Sabine I', the night he nearly died.

"No," she murmured, struggling to sit up. Philippe's hands were in the air as Bartzyk pointed a gun at his chest, "no," she repeated, "I can't lose you again."

"Mon coeur," Philippe murmured, wrapping his arm around her waist and helping her to her feet, "that will not happen." He smiled, wiping a trickle of blood from the corner of her mouth. "Remember what you told me earlier," he whispered.

Sabine stared up at him. "I want to die with you."

"Touching, very touching," Bartzyk sneered, "so touching that I am going to grant Miss Jouey her request," he pointed his gun at them, "I will kill both of you."

"You fool," Professor Dumere murmured, shaking his head, "we are all going to die."

"What?" Bartzyk bellowed, turning to the Professor, "what are you talking about?"

"My research; do you think I would let a madman such as yourself use it for his own personal gain?"

Bartzyk laughed. "My dear Professor, I did not say I would use it—I said I wanted it, to wield power." His pale eyes glittered. "Think of it! A Doomsday Machine! Capable of destroying all life on earth! Owning a weapon of that magnitude would make me invincible!"

Professor Dumere smiled sadly. "Which is why I destroyed it."

"What?" Bartzyk bellowed. "When?"

"This afternoon, at Mission Control, when I saw your airplane land and your henchmen with their guns storm the compound. I contacted the Aquarius and gave instructions to my scientists," he paused, "I told them to destroy the research and evacuate the lab."

"I don't believe you!" Bartzyk roared, the veins on his thick neck throbbing, "you wouldn't destroy decades of work!"

"I would," the Professor said softly, "and I did."

"You're bluffing," Bartzyk sneered, "you would say anything to save the lives of the people you love."

The Professor smiled, gazing at Sabine and Philippe, who were standing on the edge of the deck, their arms wrapped around each others' waists. "It is true, I love them both, but I would never allow my work to be corrupted by a savage…"

"Savage?" Bartzyk turned and pointed his gun at Professor Dumere. "You dare call me a…"

Suddenly a low rumble from below reverberated and crescendoed into a roar. The calm sea exploded, the ocean gurgling and churning as the Aquarius ripped apart. Waves washed over the deck of the buoy, sending Bartzyk's shrieking men into the violent swell. Bartzyk, startled, lost his footing as he turned to Philippe and Sabine. "At least I will have the satisfaction," Bartzyk roared, pointing his gun at them as he clung to the life lines on the sailboat, "of seeing you both die!"

"Jump!" Philippe screamed as four shots rang out in the darkness.

Wave after wave pounded the buoy, the bell atop clanging an unheeded warning. The 'Sabine II', listing on its side, shuddered and sank, swallowed up by the furious sea.

THIRTY TWO

"Yes, sir, Professor Dumere was found on Key Largo; he'd washed ashore in a dinghy," Heinrich Gruber adjusted his straw hat and sipped his drink, "yes, sir, alive but quite disorientated. He doesn't remember what happened…no, sir, no sign of either of them or Bartzyk…two bodies washed up but they were identified as Bartzyk's henchmen…yes, sir, it is a tragedy."

Forty eight hours had passed since the explosion that destroyed the Aquarius research lab. Gruber had landed in Key Largo that morning to access the damage, spending the day inspecting the remains of the Mission Control Center and the debris littered ocean surrounding the Life Support Buoy. The sun was setting over the bay as Gruber, lounging in an aqua beach chair at the hotel pool, sipped his drink and filed his report with the Chairman of the Company.

"Yes, sir, I surveyed the Mission Control Center,

or what's left of it; it appears all of the Professor's research was destroyed…yes, sir, a pity we weren't able to reach him first but we did try…at this point we don't know, sir, we are still sorting through the rubble…there is evidence of a small plane landing… no, sir, it is gone…Sir, I don't understand…ten million dollars disappeared from Bartzyk's bank account in Freeport?" Gruber smiled slyly. "Yes, sir the electronic transfer will be difficult to trace, but not impossible…yes, sir, I'll be back in Paris in a few days." Gruber gazed at a blonde woman who was sipping a drink at the bar; she felt his gaze and smiled. "Sir, perhaps it would be better if I spent the entire week here, just to make sure all of the loose ends are tied up," Gruber adjusted his hat and smiled back. "Of course, sir, I will keep you informed of any further developments…very good…ciao."

Gruber snapped his cell phone shut and slipped it into the breast pocket of his Hawaiian print shirt. He stood up and strolled across the pool patio, glancing at his reflection in the mirror behind the bar.

"Pardon, me," Gruber smiled into the bright blue eyes of the blonde woman who smiled back, "how is it possible that a beautiful woman like you is drinking alone? Am I dreaming?"

She laughed gaily. "I am not a dream."

"But you are." Gruber pulled out a stool. "May I buy you a drink?"

"Certainly," she chirped, "this is my first day here; I'm from Milwaukee and I cannot tell you how happy I am to be where it's warm," she paused and smiled at Gruber. "Are you here for the weather?"

"Of course," Gruber motioned to the bartender, "I am here for the weather."

EPILOGUE

Two months later, somewhere in French Polynesia

The sun was setting over the turquoise ocean, painting the sky in streaks of red and orange as it disappeared from the endless horizon. Violet clouds billowed atop the layers of fire, as wisps of pink colored the blue above. A soft wind scented with frangipani whispered through the palm fronds as the small fishing boats bobbed up and down in the gentle sea.

Apart from the small fishing vessels, a forty foot sailboat stood alone, its majestic structure impervious to the whims of the tide. A light shone inside on a dark haired woman sitting at a table. She was smiling up at a man who was pouring wine into her glass. He laughed as she stroked his bare back. Cupping her face in his hand he bent to kiss her, her arm wrapping around his neck.

Outside, atop the sailboat's mainmast, a French flag fluttered in the evening breeze; on the port side, painted in red, 'Sabine III'.

Special thanks to

Ms. Carolyn Waters, The New York Society Library
Mr. Thomas Potts, Director, Aquarius Research Laboratory

Cover photo
Moorea sunset, French Polynesia
©istockphoto.com/Lehnhoff